FOR WHOM THE BELL TOLLS

FOR WHOM THE BELL TOLLS

PROTECTED BY THE DAMNED, BOOK 8

MICHAEL TODD   MICHAEL ANDERLE
LAURIE STARKEY

DISRUPTIVE IMAGINATION

LMBPN Publishing
PMB 196, 2540 South Maryland Pkwy
Las Vegas, NV 89109

First US edition, June 2018
Version 1.03, June 2018

FOR WHOM THE BELL TOLLS TEAM

Beta Readers

Dorothy Lloyd
Tom Dickerson
Dorene Johnson
Diane Velasquez
Timothy Cox
Sarah Weir

JIT Readers

Kelly O'Donnell
James Caplan
John Ashmore
Peter Manis
Larry Omans
Paul Westman

If we missed anyone, please let us know!

Weapons Consultant
John Kern
Proprietor
Spurlock's - Henderson NV

Editor
Lynne Stiegler

DEDICATION

To Family, Friends and
Those Who Love
to Read.
May We All Enjoy Grace
to Live the Life We Are
Called.

— Michael Anderle

K atie rolled her shoulders as she looked out over the lawn of the old Wyoming hotel. There were bodies strewn across the grass, some friend, some foe. Pandora was quiet, and Katie could tell she was worn out after taking over her body and fighting so many demons.

It had definitely been interesting not being in control of her own body, but now she knew without a doubt at that point that she could trust Pandora to give control back. To not go running off with her body and wreak havoc on humanity.

Or on random donut shops the world over.

Don't bet on it. Pandora's soft laugh barely registered in her brain.

"You okay?" Damian stared at her for a moment, looking her over as if he expected Pandora to pop back out and sashay over to him.

She looked up. "I'm fine. Just a little spent, that's all." She looked around. "Who are we waiting for?"

"General Brushwood. He's finishing up his briefing from the colonel about what happened out here. We'll have to go through it inside."

"But..."

"Don't worry, I got it covered, I know you don't have much of a memory of any of it. But let me ask you something..." Damian turned to face her, lowering his voice and raising an eyebrow. "What did it *feel* like?"

She matched his lowered voice. "Initially it felt like a rush of heat and a whole lot of power surging through me, then it was calm—like sleep."

"Interesting. Well, I'm glad she gave you back. Our team wouldn't be right without you."

Katie chuckled. "Thanks, but this body is a lot less busty."

I can fix that, Pandora whispered in a weak voice.

Back off the boobies, sister. I got enough.

"I have no comment." Damian smiled as General Brushwood returned the colonel's salute and started across the grass toward them. "Just relax."

Katie smiled. "Loose as a goose."

Now who's disgusting?

It's just a saying, Katie replied.

He nodded to them both. "Thanks for sticking around. These briefings can take a while, especially after a battle like this one." The general walked them away from the others. "You guys saved a lot of lives today, and I want to thank you for that. One casualty is *nothing*, compared to what a fight like this would have cost us six months ago."

Damian frowned and shook his head. "For us, sir, one is one too many, but we are doing the best we can. I think that the military *will* be able to learn from us—as we will from them—on future missions." He looked at Katie.

"Absolutely, and the support they gave us was great. It would have been a lot tougher without them."

The general nodded and stood up a bit straighter. "We have some good men on these teams. I know that when the next battle comes they will be ready for it. So, let's get down to the nitty-gritty here. Tell me what happened from your side."

Damian gestured to Katie and she ran through her thoughts, rewinding from before Pandora took over. Everything after was still kind of a blur.

"We landed on that hill up there and moved down and around the perimeter. The troops stayed back until we were at the front. Damian and I crouched at the edge of the woods and saw two demons closing in behind us. They hadn't seen us yet and I was able to swing back around and come up behind them, and I took them out before they became a problem. One body was found by the troops. After that we snuck over to that woodshed, and...um...re-grouped." Katie looked at Damian.

Damien nodded. "Agreed. We went over strategy once again. Going in through the front door was going to be risky, so we wanted to make sure we were ready. From there we moved in through the front door, finding it some-what vacant. The demons had spread out through the hotel, so we went room to room until we found demons or infected and took them out."

"Why didn't you split up?" The general glanced at Katie, noticing how quiet she had gotten. Since she was usually the primary on takedowns, it seemed slightly odd that Damian was going through the brief.

Damien shrugged. "Seeing as the hotel is so large and we weren't sure what kind of danger awaited, four hands seemed smarter than two."

"I see."

"So Katie and I went through, taking a few demons down in the different rooms and then Katie took down some larger ones in the kitchen and down the hall. When you do a walk-through of the area you will see the piles of dust where the demons fell."

"Right, and that was when the colonel took over—when the demons fled into the yard."

"Yes." Damian nodded, glancing at Katie who gave a tight-lipped smile.

"Right then, so let me ask: what was the portal? Who was behind that?"

"Our suspicion is that it's a major demon." Katie glanced at the place the portal had opened. "One of the top Eight, and we also believe he is the leader of this group of mercenaries. We think he is the one teaching them every-thing, and he is capable of opening and closing portals to Earth."

The general took off his cover and scratched the top of his head. "That *is* alarming."

Katie nodded in agreement. "It's the same way they got through at our old base, only that demon wasn't quite as strong. If he had been, I wouldn't have been able to push him back through."

With my *car.* Pandora growled in Katie's head.

He looked at them. "Do you believe this will continue to be an issue?"

"I do." Katie nodded. "I believe that until these top demons are taken care of, they will continue to escalate the situation. It seems dire, I know, but we just have to stay vigilant. I think we have put a damn good hurting on their troops, so it will take them a moment to regroup. Which is good, because..." She sighed. "We need one too."

The general looked over his shoulder at one of his guards, who tapped his watch. He turned back to Katie and Damian and shook their hands. "I have to get going, but good work today. You were an asset beyond measure. I'll be in touch."

Katie and Damian nodded and the general was escorted back to his chopper. Two guards rode with him and two remained on the ground to wait for the helo to take off. Katie put her hand on her stomach and let out a deep breath.

Damian chuckled and turned toward her. "You didn't think I'd out you to the general, did you? He might have had an aneurysm right where he stood."

Katie snickered. "I could have just flashed him Pandora boob and things would have been all good in the world."

Damn straight, Pandora grumbled.

Two soldiers walked past Katie and Damian, patting them on the shoulder and somberly nodding in thanks. The military were busy taking care of the dead, including their own. They looked both sad and angry, but that was how it was for them. That a comrade had fallen pissed them off no end, building the desire for revenge.

Katie couldn't lie; she had felt that urge all too recently

as well. Right then, though, she just wanted to get back to base, unwind, and see her family again.

The five Killers presently at the base were sitting around a table in the meeting room.

"The intel I've pulled so far has revealed a number of these energy surges over the last few weeks." Timothy took a sip of his Cherry Coke.

"And you think these larger surges have been portals?" Stephanie looked at Timothy through narrowed eyes. "Portals to *hell*?"

His slurping was making her teeth vibrate.

"That's what the intel says, yes."

Calvin spoke from Timothy's right. "Do you have the ability to see these portal surges in real time?"

"You bet your tight ass I do," Timothy replied. "Like the one during the battle today—I saw it clear as day."

"That's good." Stephanie pursed her lips and her eyes moved over the room as she thought. "That means if we are in battle and one of these opens you can call it down to us."

"*Finally* they are catching on." Timothy put his arms in the air and looked at the ceiling with sarcasm in his voice. "We will be able to see all these little pops of energy in real time."

Stephanie smirked and nodded. "And *that* will give us

time to kick ass before their feet hit the ground."

"You got *that* right, sister." Timothy high-fived her across the table. She laughed and looked at Calvin, who raised an eyebrow and shook his head.

"All right, then let's conclude this ops meeting until Damian and Katie return. Unless you have something else to add, Korbin?"

Korbin looked like he was in a daze. "No, I'm good."

Calvin, Stephanie, Korbin, Eric, and Timothy stood up and Timothy gathered his papers. Calvin watched him for a moment; the boy was more relaxed than when he had first gotten to the base. Still annoying as hell, but at least he was working as part of the team.

"Good job today, Timmy."

Timothy smiled. "Thanks, Calvin."

Timothy's shoulders relaxed as they left the room. It had been a while since he'd felt anything like that and he was starting to think that maybe being a part of the team wouldn't be so bad. He collected his things and headed down the tunnel to his room.

He sat down on the edge of his bed and fixed his eyes on the floor, thinking about his place on the team. He had never really belonged to anything like it before.

Inside his mind though, Mr. Toss-Cold-Water-on-his-Thoughts spoke again. *While you 're off in Happy Rainbow Land right now, all I can think about are the tits on that Stephanie character. Well, those, mixed with her spicy little tie-me-up, tie-me-*

down personality. *Yes, son, that* is *exactly the kind of woman this incubus needs. Bring me some of that! She can even bring a whip.*

Timothy rolled his eyes and sighed. *And to think that for just a minute I had forgotten you were there, festering inside me like an infection.*

Get used to it. We are a duo from now on.

Until I learn how to control you, that is. Besides, I kind of like working with people. It's not so lonely anymore. And I am not ruining that by sleeping with any of them, and definitely not one of the women.

His demon whined, *It's not like I have much of a choice. I mean, my options are very limited. We have the spicy one, but she's fucking taken by Mr. Snoreworthy, and Katie, who is* hell-no-terrifying *on every level.* Timothy could just about feel his demon pouting. *This sucks.*

What is it with you and Katie? I mean, sure, she's one tough bitch, but she's not that *scary. Who is this demon inside of her? Don't think I don't notice how you shrivel up into a ball every time she comes around. It makes me want to tag along with her whenever possible just to get you to shut the hell up.*

She's a scary bitch, that's all I'm going to say about it. His demon shivered, making the hair on Timothy's arms stand up straight.

Aw, wittle demon talks such a big game, but some woman comes around and he pisses his demon panties.

Timothy's demon chuckled. *Keep messing with me and you'll find yourself waking up in some Vegas hotel room surrounded by naked women, and every one of them will have been fucked to exhaustion.*

Timothy shuddered and shut up. The last thing he wanted was to change teams. He liked big strong men, even if his demon was throwing him a curve ball in every five seconds. He sighed and leaned back on his bed.

It's not like you have to worry about dick anyway. All these men bat for the other team. Apparently gay Damned are rare.

Good! his incubus retorted.

His demon settled in, tired of talking about it. He was not going to let Timothy have his way, and he definitely wouldn't be going anywhere near that crazy bitch-demon in Katie.

Timothy laid there staring up at the ceiling, thinking about the work he had done. This had been the first time he had used his skills for anything other than hacking or stealing. He had done some serious shit that day, and he wasn't going to let the incubus fuck with him.

He would have never thought being on the right side of things would feel good. Where he had come from had been like a prison, but here everyone acted like family.

This was definitely the other side of the tracks for him.

He sat up on the bed and pulled his shoes back on, then stared up at his reflection in the mirror and wrinkled his nose. He was not going to keep looking like some scrub just because there were no eligible men around. He marched out of his room, ignoring his demon—who had caught on to what he was going to do.

Don't you dare," the demon growled.

Timothy knocked on Stephanie's door and waited for her to answer. She opened the door and peered at Timothy, who had mischief in his eyes. "What can I do for you?"

"Girl, I need a makeover stat."

Stephanie smirked. "Now that is *definitely* something I can handle. Come into my magic room of beauty." She stepped to the side, rubbing her hands together. "What did you have in mind?"

Timothy flounced into the room and executed a catwalk turn, then put his hand up to his hair. He fluffed it as he swirled his head from side to side.

"First I need to do something about this mop, then I need to get into town and buy myself some new clothes." He waved a hand up and down his body. "This prison uniform is *not* doing me any favors in the looks department."

Stephanie giggled and put her hand on her chin, eyeing his white t-shirt, blue jeans, and Keds. She hadn't seen that uniform before, but he was right—he kind of looked like he was on work-release. She went over to her dresser to grab her makeup bag, slowly pulling out her scissors and a comb. She pulled her desk chair into her bathroom and set him down in front of the mirror with a towel around his neck, and another on the floor to catch the hair.

He raised an eyebrow when Stephanie withdrew a pair of clippers from a drawer.

She explained, "I was having an existential crisis once and thought about shaving the whole thing, although I stopped myself."

"Thank God." He sighed. "So what is your plan? I know you have one."

Timothy's demon sniffed the air and laughed. *"This hottie used to be a madam!"*

Timothy gasped and began to fan himself. "Girl, my demon just told me you used to be a madam."

Stephanie smiled. "Sweetie, that is only the beginning. Let me just tell you..."

2

The helo landed on the base's landing pad, its rotors slowing down after the pilot shut off the engine. Katie stepped out and sand hit her black leather boots. She ducked as she cleared the landing pad, then waited on the side with her bag in her hand as Damian thanked the pilot and caught up with her.

They were both exhausted, Katie more so after the change she had gone through. However, after the two of them rode the elevator down and the doors opened on their waiting friends, she was happy to see them dressed to go out. Time with her family was *exactly* what she needed.

Stephanie clapped for everyone's attention. "We're headed to Torn Asunder. A little booze, a little food, and a *whole* lot of family."

Korbin smiled as he tucked his blue button-up shirt into the back of his pants. "Go get ready. We'll wait here for you."

Katie nodded and glanced at a guy standing near the

back, doing a double-take when she realized it was Timothy. He looked different now; clean shaven, hair cut, and wearing actual clothes instead of the jeans and issue white t-shirt he'd had on when last she had seen him. He looked at her and smiled, raking his hand through his former-but-now-missing long hair. Katie laughed and nodded in approval as she headed off to change her clothes.

Nachos, Pandora stated. *I'm in the mood for some of those fucking terrible-but-I-have-to-eat-one-more Torn Asunder nachos.*

Sounds good to me, but they'd better not go to my tits. These things are getting hard to carry around.

Katie dressed in a pair of jeans and tight black V-neck shirt before meeting the others in the garage, all loaded up ready to go.

They jumped into the SUV and headed out, Damian taking his spot behind the wheel with Korbin next to him. Stephanie sat in the middle section between Katie and Timothy, and Calvin sprawled in the back seat, leaving Eric squished into the corner giving him the stink eye.

They talked and laughed all the way there, and took one of the few empty tables inside. Everybody ordered a drink and Korbin took the stage for the first time ever.

He cleared his throat and tapped the mic, clearly uncomfortable with public speaking. "I just wanted to get up here and talk for a moment about the most recent battle. Luckily for us—this time—none of the Damned lost their lives, but we did lose one of our allies. To give us a chance to reflect on that, I'm gonna put Katie on the spot and bring her up here. Katie?"

Katie sighed and made her way to the stage with a beer

in her hand. She stuck her tongue out at Korbin as she passed him and he chuckled.

She took the mic with her free hand and looked out at the faces in the crowd. "Damn! Things have been crazy over the last few months. So many lives lost, but so many saved as well."

"Hear, hear," someone yelled from the small crowd.

"One thing we've never done is honor those fallen heroes who fight with us without any of our advantages. In my opinion, their bravery makes them all the more deserving of a tribute. I'm talking about the men and women of the Armed Services who fight the demons with no special powers and no super-strength, just the weapons in their hands and the courage in their hearts. So many of them have made the ultimate sacrifice, yet still the teams keep going out there and *kicking ass!*"

The crowd cheered and raised their beers.

Katie raised hers in salute. "*This* is to all of those who have served, fought, and died for the cause. *You* are the heroes this world needs: the unselfish, the brave, and the mighty. This is to all of you who have died by the claws of demons. Joseph Campbell once said, 'A hero is someone who has given his or her life to something bigger than oneself.' You will *never* be forgotten."

Everyone clinked their glasses together and drank to the memories of their brave allies.

Katie got down off the stage and sat back down at the table with Calvin and Korbin. Korbin patted her on the back and nodded, tapping his glass to hers. The waitress arrived with trays of food and set a giant plate of nachos in front of her.

Katie could almost feel Pandora rubbing her hands together and drooling.

Three tables down an argument broke out, and everyone but Timothy picked their plates and lifted their drinks into the air. He watched the fighting for several moments, then glanced down at the tape holding up their table. He lifted his plate and drink just as the fight came to them and two guys crashed through their table.

Katie, Calvin, Stephanie, Eric, Damian, and Korbin cheered, nodding in approval at Timothy for paying attention. The two guys stood up, one helping the other to his feet. The blond looked at Timothy and smiled ruefully.

"Sorry, man."

Timothy gave him a cheeky wink. "Oh, it's all right, sweetie. You can fall into my lap *any* time."

The guy gave him a funny look and walked back to his table. The crew looked at each other and burst into laughter and the bartender scurried out and set another table over the broken one.

Timothy put his plate down and nodded. "Bet he won't land on *this* table again."

Stephanie patted him on the back. "We got us a smart one here, ladies and gents."

Calvin held up his glass. "Quick thinking on that plate. Mine was a pile of ass-nachos the first time it happened to me."

"Mine was ass-spaghetti," Korbin raised his glass chuckling.

Katie laughed. "I don't remember what it was, but it left me hungry—and that is *never* a good thing to do to me *or* my demon."

Korbin nodded in agreement.

Stephanie slapped her lover in the stomach. "Don't let this one fool you. He is a grumpy asshole even *without* a hungry demon."

"Truth." Calvin chuckled, raising his glass.

They laughed and talked for the rest of the evening, bringing Timothy into the family and enjoying the normality for as long as they could.

They knew that it wouldn't be long before another call came and another soul was lost, but all they had was right now. Everything that had happened to that point had forged them into the family they were, following each other to hell and back every time.

They weren't going to take that for granted.

Moloch's wicked scaled claws ran gently over the tiny flickering souls that lined his office fireplace and they collectively shrieked like the crackle of a fire on a cold night.

It was everything he could do not to rip a hole in the building. He was *livid*—completely appalled by how the battle had gone—but given the clearing throats and chattering teeth behind him blowing up would only frighten his remaining troops—and he needed them to go back out there.

Trenton looked at the survivors, bruised, bloody, and clinging to the last bit of bravery as they stood in the pits of hell. Sweat poured from their foreheads, and they clasped their hands together tightly. He shook his head, half disappointed in their weakness, the other half ready to get back out there and fix what they had screwed up.

"Your Eminence, if I may—"

"You may *not!*" Moloch roared. He slammed his fist against the wall, causing pieces of stone to crumble to the floor.

Trenton took a step back toward the others. He knew that pushing Moloch would do no good. It could even possibly get him and his brothers cast into the depths of hell forever.

He wasn't ready to die, not when there was revenge to be had. And now he had a *reason* to hate. He had a *reason* for revenge, and he wanted to go after it.

Moloch sighed and calmed himself, then straightened to tower above the others. He turned to the Enlightened mercenary and stroked the long black hair coming from his chin. He had to remember that no matter how little he cared for them, *they* didn't need to know that.

"I take part of the blame for this." Moloch put up his hand to stop Trenton from interrupting. "I underestimated the Damned. This other team is playing with a heavy-weight. They are not just some humans Damned by low-level demons. They are strong—stronger than any of you— and some of them rival even the highest-level demons like T'Chezz. We will need to do some research before we plan another battle, but for now I will send you back to prepare. This time you will train harder and longer, eat *only* what is necessary, keep to yourselves, and stay off of the radar."

Trenton waited for a moment to make sure Moloch was finished. "How will we know when it is time?"

"I will come to you." Moloch stood in front of Trenton. "I need you to listen carefully. You will get your revenge—the desire for which I can *smell* coming from your pores—but you will *not* move on these Damned until I say so. Then and only then will you have a chance of defeating these mercenaries and their human allies. Do you understand me?"

Trenton lowered his head. "Yes. How can we reach you if we need you?"

"I will be watching you, and I will appear if I think you truly need my guidance. Now, I am sending you survivors back, and I will send the demons into new bodies once I pull them from the depths of hell. In the meantime, do not *share* this information with anyone. I do not need another reckless following to dispose of."

Trenton looked up quickly, thinking about everyone who had gathered to call Moloch down in the beginning. "Dispose of?"

"Of course," Moloch sneered. "You didn't think they could see me, know what our plan was, and still live, did you? Don't worry, their souls are securely and specially placed down here with me, right where they wanted to be. Now go!"

Moloch stretched his arms wide, tearing a hole in midair to create a portal back to Earth, and the survivors walked through.

He walked to the fireplace and smiled at the captive dancing souls. "Isn't that right, my puny human souls? I put you right where I promised—in this little box for my pleasure...

"For *eternity.*"

Moloch's deep laugh carried through the halls of the building and out to the dark fiery lava fields.

Back on Earth, Trenton swore he heard that deep menacing laugh as he brushed the soot from his pants.

That laugh was his only ticket to revenge, and Trenton knew it.

Katie whistled as she walked into the kitchen carrying three pink pastry boxes, which she set on the table. She then pulled out three bottles of water out of the fridge and loaded them into her pack. It was a beautiful clear day outside so she wasn't going to waste it training in the deep recesses of the tunnels.

She needed air and freedom, and she needed to be alone with her thoughts—"her thoughts" meaning Pandora, in this instance.

She zipped her bag and turned to grab the donuts, finding Calvin and Eric in back of her. Eric snuck to the side and opened a box, but Katie lunged forward and slapped his hand. He yelped in surprise.

Calvin put his hands up in surrender and was about to back away when her eyes swiveled in his direction. He advised Eric, "I wouldn't touch her donuts if I were you."

"He knows me well." Katie flashed Calvin a smile and picked up the three boxes, then paused for a moment. She sighed and put one back on the table and nodded at Eric.

"Where you goin' this morning?" Calvin grabbed a donut, eating half in one bite.

"Going to the cliff to get some practice in, but I need my sugar fix."

Eric lifted an eyebrow. "With that much sugar you will be practicing for the next three days non-stop."

Calvin grinned. "That or she'll come back with even bigger boobs."

Katie laughed shaking her head. "This is just a snack for Pandora, and she will make sure I work off every ounce of it before I come back here. She doesn't play when it comes to training."

Damn right, and by the way, the big guy could use some training. He gets out of breath in a heartbeat.

Katie smirked as she glanced at Calvin.

"What? What did she say about me?"

"*Noooothing.*" Katie laughed.

"Oh, *hell* no! You tell that Pandora she better back off or face these guns!" Calvin pushed up his sleeves and flexed his muscles, which by most standards were pretty impressive.

Pandora giggled, having gotten *exactly* what she'd wanted. Katie just shook her head and laughed.

Calvin slowly put down his arms. "I gave her exactly what she wanted, didn't I?"

Yep, Pandora snickered.

"Yep!" Katie yelled back as she strolled down the tunnel toward the elevator.

You should cut him some slack, Pandora. He's like your biggest fan, and he hasn't even seen your gigantic boobs.

Nah, messing with him is the best. He hasn't seen my gigantic boobs and I haven't seen that gigantic black-man schlong, so I guess that makes us equal. Maybe next time I take you over I'll take advantage of his weakness.

No. Absolutely not! So help me, if I wake up in bed with him you will never come out to play again.

I don't know, it might be worth it. I mean, seriously—everything is bigger in...a black man's pants.

It's Texas. "Everything is bigger in Texas," Katie corrected.

Shit, then what are we doing here?

Katie laughed and walked into the training area, going to the weapons case and pulling out her staff. She made sure the latch was tight and pushed it into the new backstrap she had ordered. The leg straps were just too bulky, and they slowed her down. This was much easier to maneuver.

She picked up her boxes again and headed to the elevator, whistling as she went. When the doors opened to the outside she smiled, feeling the warmth of the sun on her face. She took her keys from the box inside the garage and slid her hand across her truck's paint.

Katie patted the vehicle. "Hey, girl, sorry I haven't been around for a while to take you out, but today changes all that."

I still miss the car.

I still miss the simple life, but you can't always get what you want.

Pandora smirked. *Bet me.*

3

K atie stuck her hand out of the open window as she cruised over the sand dunes and savored the wind blowing through her hair as she made her way to the mountainous part of their land. She couldn't help but think about her old teammate Jeremy and how badly he would have freaked if he'd seen Pandora take over.

He would have melted into a puddle at her feet in two seconds.

Katie smiled, putting her hand back on the wheel as she approached the upward slope. She drove the truck up far enough to find a good place to park and hiked up the rest of the way.

When she got to the top with her bag and the two boxes of donuts she was ever-so-slightly out of breath. She set everything down and put her hands on her lower back, arching her back. She couldn't even see her toes anymore. Her boobs were too big and her bra straps were pulling.

If you are going to make my boobs this big, would you at least keep up with the maintenance? I'm gonna need metal cables to keep these suckers up soon, and my back is killing me.

Picky, picky, Pandora grumbled. *Hold on.*

Pandora sniffed around for a moment and out of nowhere Katie felt almost complete relief. Her breasts were lighter and perkier, although they didn't change in size at all. She nodded, impressed, and bounced up and down on her toes, and her tits stayed firmly in place.

That's *what I'm talkin' about. Why didn't you do that from the beginning?*

You are an impossible human. Now, give me a donut and pull out your staff—it's time to rock 'n roll.

Yes, ma'am!

There was a small pause and a snicker. *I said "staff!"*

Katie chuckled to herself and grabbed a glazed donut from the box. Pandora tsked at her, so she returned it and took a cream-filled one instead. "Okay, but if I puke it's on you."

Technically it's on Mother Nature, but I got this. Don't you worry.

Katie ate the donut, rolling her eyes as Pandora oohed and ahhed at the taste. When she was done, she licked her fingers, picked up her staff, and held it out in front of her with both hands. She swung it and started moving through her warmup kata.

She was surprised at how fluid and easy it felt.

The first time she had tripped all over the place, hitting her ankles with the staff. Now she could move without thinking of what was next, as if her body were programmed. It was a freeing feeling, and one that could not be explained.

She felt at one with her staff.

After about thirty minutes of warmup Pandora kicked in, giving her new moves to practice to take her to the next level.

To be really good at this you have got to focus. Clear your mind, stop thinking about all the demons you are gonna kill, and stop thinking about blades that retract. Just let the movements take you.

Katie closed her eyes and slowly let out her breath, becoming aware of the pole in her hands. She wove around the rocky terrain in offensive moves, just practicing how to attack fluidly with the weapon. When she was done with that, she stopped to grab the next donut and chowed it down.

Now, I'm going to teach you the Chatan Yara No Kon Sho, *which is a simple kata. I'll move you along the first time, then I want you to take over.*

Did you have anything to do with making this up?

No comment.

Katie nodded and stood up straight with her staff vertical at her side. Her arm pushed the staff straight out and turned it in her right hand, then she lunged to the left, breathing steadily.

She took the top of her staff in her left hand and quickly twisted it down, jabbing outwards with a grunt. She turned the staff in a circular disarming motion before stepping forward with one foot in front of the other to stab outward repeatedly. She stepped back, twirling the end of the staff around again before twisting to the right. She repeated the series to the right, and then jabbed outward. Her feet moved quickly as she batted the staff ends front and back like she was swatting an opponent in the ribs. She raised the staff over her head and thrust it downward, imagining a demon head beneath it.

Sweat poured from Katie's forehead as she thrust and jabbed over and over with the staff. She could only imagine how painful it would be to be jabbed in the stomach, especially if the blades were out.

She walked forward, moving the staff up and down and side to side, then stopped and went back in the other direction. She swiveled and dropped to one knee, pushing the staff under her arm, then rose and twirled the staff over her head like a helicopter, then jabbed up and down and forward once again.

With each move Pandora would yell, and the sounds echoed off the cliffs.

To finish the kata she lifted the staff by the end like a lightsaber and swatted from side to side. Her arms moved faster than she would have thought possible and she lifted one leg and yelled, bashing the stick to the ground. Slowly she stood up straightened, the staff again parallel with her side. As soon as she had bowed Pandora released her body.

Katie was breathing heavily, so she set the staff down and chugged a bottle of water.

Wow, that was intense.

It's a good one. You'll be able to kick serious ass when you get it down.

Have you used that move before?

Hell, yeah I have, though I don't want to reveal on whom.

You used it on humans, didn't you?

Pandora sighed deeply in Katie's mind. *How about another donut?*

Katie shook her head, picked up another donut, and took a bite. *You* do *know I am aware you weren't some kind of angel before you came into my body. I know you would have sooner eaten my heart than become my friend back in the day.*

Still would. Pandora chuckled. *But yes, I know you know that. I just feel a bit ashamed now, although I don't know if it's because I am helping the enemy or because I* want *to help the enemy.*

Uh-oh, someone is growing a conscience.

Don't go crazy now! I still might get out of this body one day and have you for an afternoon snack.

All my plastic surgery will poison you.

Good point. Pandora laughed and then grew a bit thoughtful. *I wonder if your tits taste like donuts?*

That's disgusting! Katie growled. *And yet, it's a valid question.*

Katie sat down on one of the boulders and spread her legs in front of her, then leaned back and drank the rest of the bottle.

She put her head back and let the breeze cool her sweaty body. She was always relaxed when she trained up here, at least since Jeremy died. Sometimes she felt like a piece of him was still on the hill.

Where do you think we will land at the end of all this? Katie asked.

Sheesh, who knows? I've learned over the years that nothing ever turns out how you think it will, and especially not the way you want *it. I've seen so many ups and downs that sometimes I'm glad to get banished to the depths of hell. Not so many screaming souls down there, and the heads of the joint shut up for a couple hundred years. It's like a really fucking hot vacation.*

Um, I have a request.

Uh-oh.

Since I am now allowing you to take over my body—which takes a hell of a lot of trust, by the way—I want to know something about you.

The biggest dick was...

No, not that. Katie grimaced. *I want to know who you really are, where you came from, and when you came back to Earth.*

Pandora sighed and was quiet for a moment. *All right, I guess it's about time you knew. And it's only fair, since they are all after me and thus after you as well.*

Truth. Katie sighed.

My real name is Lilith. I am—or was—Lucifer's wife.

Holy shit! Katie jumped up from her stone and looked around as though she expected the devil himself to step out from behind a rock.

Calm down, honey, he won't be showing up any time soon.

You are Lucifer's wife? You are Mrs. Devil Incarnate? I mean, I knew you were crazy powerful but I had no idea.

Pandora spoke normally. *It's really not that big a deal.*

Katie's head bobbed. *Uh, yes? Yes, it is.*

Okay, it is, but it's not like I wanted to be his wife. I wanted a divorce, remember?

He's just gonna chill down there on his skull throne and take that lying down?

You really have no idea what hell is like. Try a huge office with a view, and he personally can't do anything about it. He can't come to Earth. If he does the angels will be down here so fast your bibles will flame up. They will kick his motherfucking ass so far away he'd dissipate. I guess you could consider him to be under house arrest, only instead of an ankle bracelet he has the biggest and baddest team of angels tracking his every breath.

I thought God chained him up?

You humans take things so literally. That's just your interpretation, because it helps you sleep at night. He might as well be chained up though, especially if your only other option is death.

So you decided you didn't want to be the hell queen. Why?

Actually I was known as the Queen of Perdition, but most called me "Gehenna" or "Queen Lilith." And hell, the perks were pretty sweet—fresh flesh all the time, hot men everywhere, and I don't just mean that literally.

Katie smirked as Pandora continued.

I just didn't want to be with him anymore. I wanted my freedom, and you can imagine marrying a convict—it's a life of seclusion. I don't like to be roped down.

When did you decide all that? Sitting in your high-rise hell-condo overlooking Fire and Brimstone Park?

Cute. Pandora snorted. *No, it happened recently—since I came up this last time.*

Shit, that's some heavy stuff. Katie frowned, taking another a donut out of the box. *I imagine that once you've been the Devil's wife there aren't too many more powerful men you could have your eye on.*

Oh, sweetie, think about the royals in England. Parliament makes the rulings; the queen just waves and smiles. There are much more powerful devils out there. Lucifer lost his sheen a long time ago, and he's wallowing in self-pity. Don't get me wrong, he could wipe us all out with one swoop of his scaly red arms, but he's too busy being the one everyone fears. Gets old after a while.

I bet. Katie bit into her donut. *The last guy I slept with died the next day, if that makes you feel any better.*

It does, Pandora deadpanned. *In fact, I would consider maybe closing your damn legs. You don't want to go killing all the hot men.*

Katie gasped. *Oh my God!*

I'm just kidding. Pandora laughed. *You are so sensitive.*

That was not cool, bitch. Not cool at all. Katie took another bite of her donut.

Was it too soon?

Jokes about dead ex-lovers have to wait at least like...two years.

Kajesus, that's a bit excessive. You need to lighten up. Back home they'd be telling those jokes at the funeral.

You guys have funerals?

No, but if we did that's what would be the topic of conversation.

Great, and to think there's a chance I'll end up there!

Pandora chuckled. *At least you can't kill the dead with your vagina.*

You aren't my friend. Katie tried to hide her laugh. *So rude.*

I love you too, Pandora replied. *Now get your ass up and do that kata again. I want to hear your best karate yell.*

I'm going to start meowing every time I do it and see how much it confuses people.

"Moo" would be better.

Is that a fat joke? You can't make a fat joke after you make a dead ex-boyfriend joke.

So many rules! You will make me wish to slice my wrists and go to heaven at this pace! Pandora groaned before laughing.

Katie went back to work on her katas, performing the movements but definitely struggling the first couple of times. Her ankles were black and blue by the end, and at one point she hit her knee so hard with the staff that tears came to her eyes. She didn't feel like the Karate Kid at all; more like the kid who wiped the sweat off the mat after a meet.

But she knew she *would* get better, and she also knew that when she did she was going to be seriously dangerous.

If she didn't smack the shit out of her leg and cause those she was fighting to laugh themselves into submission.

On her next donut break—one box down—her phone, which was in her bag, started to ring. She groaned, forgetting she had brought it with her. She rummaged until she found it and read the text from Korbin. They were going to have a meeting in about an hour and she needed to attend.

"They are summoning me to a meeting of the minds." Katie dramatically yelled aloud.

Lord, if this is the best we got for a meeting of the minds the whole world is fucking doomed.

Very funny. We shall continue this training later, Mr. Miyagi.

I'll give you something to wax on, wax off.

Katie paused and pulled her eyebrows together. *I'm not sure how to interpret that. Could be terrifying, could be fun, could be both.*

I would go with "both." I'm never terrifying without at least some sort of fun thrown in there.

Good to know.

Katie dried her neck with her towel and shoved her

empty water bottles into her pack, then grabbed donut boxes and headed back down the hill at a jog, jumping from stone to stone and sliding down the loose gravel. She threw the trash into the back seat and tossed her bag into the passenger seat, then jumped in and sped down the mountain, laughing as she bounced all over the place.

Nothing wrong with a little afternoon drive around the dunes before business commences, right?

Seatbelt, dammit! I don't want to be stuck in your body if you are a vegetable.

4

D amian took a seat next to Katie and across from Calvin and Korbin at the round meeting table. Calvin leaned back and stared up at the ceiling as Korbin shuffled through some paperwork. It was just the four of them again, which figured since they were back to a seven-member team. They would be having management meetings instead of all-member meetings once again.

"So...the fight at the hotel." Korbin sighed as he pulled out a sheet of paper. "I read the general's briefing. One thing that confuses me is why Damian was talking so much. Aren't you usually the outspoken one while he is the Priest of Mystery?"

"I was tired." Katie popped a grape from the center of the table into her mouth.

Korbin raised an eyebrow. "Mmhmm, and since when did you two hold hands through a building, watching each other fight? Were you giving back-pats? Motivational speeches?"

"In reality, Pandora is much more than any of us knew, even me, and she is inside me. She has her secrets about her life before this, just like many of us do."

"Like what?" Calvin leaned forward. "She used to be a ballerina?"

Korbin shook his head. "I'm more interested in what that equates to on this timeline. Is she too connected? Not connected enough? Can you *really* trust her, Katie? That is ultimately what I need to know. We are putting our asses on the line each and every day, and we've put a hell of a lot of faith in your demon. I need to know we can all trust her, not just because of a gut feeling."

Man, he has it out for me today.

Damian leaned toward Katie and whispered, "Tell him what happened at the hotel."

Katie looked at him wildly.

He put his hand on her shoulder and nodded. "It is *time*."

Katie shrugged. "Mystery Priest says it's time for the big reveal, so here goes. The answer is, I am so quiet about what happened at the hotel because I don't remember how I killed those demons."

"I'm confused," Calvin replied. "Amnesia?"

"More like unconscious state," Katie mumbled. "I let Pandora fully take over my body."

Korbin's mouth dropped open and he sat there in quiet shock. Calvin dropped the pen he had been twirling through his fingers and stared at Katie for a minute.

Korbin and Calvin locked eyes and finally Calvin shrugged and shook his head.

Korbin considered his words for a moment before he spoke. "She gave your body back?"

"Obviously." Katie smirked. "Do I look like a voluptuous... You know what, scratch that. Not going there." She turned to Damian and gestured at Korbin and Calvin. "Would you please explain to these gentlemen a few of the changes I underwent to become the great Pandora?"

Damian cleared his throat and looked across the table. "Hips," he told them. "You always know it's Pandora because of her tits... I mean hips."

Bahahahaha. Pandora couldn't stop laughing.

Hey, you want to talk to these fellas? Katie asked.

Why the hell not?

"All right, boys," Katie growled, sitting forward. "Guys, meet Pandora. Pandora, say hello to the guys."

Korbin and Calvin sat perfectly still as Katie closed her eyes and relaxed into her chair.

Her body started to morph, shoulders rolling, waist cinching, and her hair growing longer. Her face changed: features becoming more prominent, her lips fuller, and her lashes longer. Her shirt stretched as her breasts enlarged, perking up even *more.*

Calvin's eyes got huge and he looked at Korbin and Pandora. Damian leaned forward and put his hand over his mouth, stifling a laugh.

He had probably been the same way the first time he saw the change, but it was amusing nonetheless.

Slowly Pandora's eyes opened. The red shining brightly and a snide smirk curled her lips.

"Well, hello there, boysssss." Her voice was luscious, lust overlaying promise and desire.

Korbin gripped the arms of his chair. "Holy shit."

"Now, the first thing you are probably noticing are these babies." Pandora pulled her arms together and shook her chest. "I'm a double D. You can tell the difference between Katie and me just by our cup size."

"So are you the entity behind Katie's...uh...sudden change of physique?" Calvin lifted an eyebrow.

"Of course! Where do you think those donuts go? I'd have her at my cup size, but Katie fights me. She says they are too large as they are."

"Breasts can be too large?" Calvin wondered aloud. Korbin and Damian turned toward him, staring at him like he said something wrong. Calvin closed his mouth and frowned. "What?"

"See!" Pandora pointed around at the guys. "You get it! I keep telling Katie that, but she just goes on complaining about back pain and not being able to see her feet or some other nonsense. I firmly believe Dolly Parton really had something going there before she scaled back."

Korbin cleared his throat and looked down at the table, amazed. "Okay, this is happening right now," he murmured to himself. "Might as well join in."

"The more the merrier, I always say." Pandora winked at Calvin.

"So you've been inside Katie since the beginning, pruning her, making her stronger, and gaining her trust. How can we know that you are being truthful?" Korbin wasn't holding back.

"Good question, and the answer is...you can't. I'm a demon, after all. But if I wanted to take Katie, I wouldn't wait for her permission. I am in here for the long haul, so

I'm not going to get her killed—which means I have to keep her friends as safe as I can too."

Korbin nodded and blew out a breath. "Fair answer."

Calvin rubbed his hands together and licked his lips, leaning forward. "So, Pandora, what do you like about Earth this time around? I'm assuming this isn't your first rodeo."

"Hardly." Pandora laughed. "But every time I come back there is something different. Clothes change, politics change, and technology changes, but humans stay the same hopeful bastards they've always been. They put so much faith in the unknown. It always baffles me, but I love to watch it. It's like a train wreck—you can't take your eyes away."

Pandora leaned back and crossed her legs, glancing at Damian and flashing him a big smile. Damian lifted an eyebrow and held up his cross, flashing a big smile back. Her smile faded to a pout and she turned back to Calvin.

"As far as what I like *this* time around? Well, we all know donuts are at the top of that list, then I suppose, soap operas, game shows—and holy shit, what the fuck is it about those Chicken Nuggets? Those fuckers are delicious, and I cannot for the life of me tell you why. I've tried over and over to figure it out, but I am still baffled."

Calvin laughed and even Korbin cracked a smile, leaning back with his hand on his chin. He was realizing after seeing Pandora in person and listening to her talk that so many things now made sense. Suddenly he understood Katie much better, and though he would never let his guard down with Pandora, he was definitely becoming more at ease with the thought of her fighting demons with the rest of them.

———

Pandora snickered, finishing a story. "So, anyway, that bitch just ran T'Chezz right over, sending the whole car to hell. That was all Katie. I had nothing to do with it."

The guys laughed for a moment and Pandora wiped the tears from the corner of her eyes. She stretched her arms into the air, a move which revealed her tight midriff, and plopped back in the chair.

"Well, boys, it's been fun, but I suppose Katie will want her body back. I'll be here if you need me. And remember, I hear *everything*."

With a wink, Pandora closed her eyes and began to morph back into Katie. Calvin shook his head, not sure he would ever get used to that. Katie opened one eye and peered down at her body and then looked at the guys, clutching her chest in relief.

She sighed in happiness. "Oh, thank God—my clothes are still on." Calvin frowned and tilted his head at her. She shook her head, feeling exhaustion start to come over her. "Nothing, nothing, never mind. Sometimes the freak inside you can be stronger than you can control. Pandora's my freak."

Calvin grinned. "That's one *hell* of a freak."

You better believe it, big guy.

———

Across the base, a table was set with a black tablecloth on one of the vacant slabs. Candles that flickered wildly in the wind, and there was a single red rose in a vase that kept threatening to blow over. The white dishes were empty since the food had been eaten, and sitting across from each other were Stephanie and Korbin, laughing about Katie's change to Pandora as they sipped some wine.

Stephanie laughed. "I can't even imagine, but it sounds like me and this bitch would get along fantastically."

"That's what I'm afraid of." Korbin lifted his glass of red wine and took a sip.

She put her glass on the tablecloth and leaned her head back to look at the bright stars overhead. They were far enough from Vegas that the night sky was absolutely amazing. She could see the Milky Way, all the constellations, and even some small planets in the distance. The breeze blew lightly over them, but wasn't cold enough to cause a chill.

"Isn't it gorgeous out here?" Stephanie cooed.

"It is." Korbin loved to watch her when she was relaxed. It was like nothing in the world could bring her down.

"I could just see it...you and me, some little house far enough from civilization to have stars like this every night but close enough to go to a bar or a show, just relaxing on our front porch."

"The dog asleep at my feet, your hand in mine..."

"The smell of lavender and roses from the garden wafting over us. Not a care in the world; completely oblivious to all this crazy shit."

Korbin took a sip of his wine. "It would be amazing."

"Oh!" Stephanie sat up in her chair. "And we could have

a big fence around the yard, and maybe a pool for skinny-dipping."

Korbin laughed. "But no one to bother us."

"That's right. We could laugh our asses off at anything we wanted, cry when we felt sad, and go for a run because we wanted to, not because we were trying to get away from something."

"We could play music through the open windows and dance barefoot in the grass, drinking wine straight out of the bottle."

Stephanie lifted her glass and laughed. "Sir, I like the way you think."

"When winter came, we could start a fire in the fireplace and curl up and listen to Christmas songs, covered with a fuzzy blanket..."

"We could make love any time we wanted, hold hands whenever, and just be *happy*."

"That would be the life, wouldn't it?" Korbin stared at her, feeling pain in his chest because those were all dreams. He didn't want to say it, though. He wanted to give her that moment; that hopeful second to let her experience it all in her mind.

Stephanie took another deep breath and opened her eyes. She reached across the tablecloth and took his hand, seeing the pain on his face even though he was trying to hide it.

She wasn't a fairytale kind of girl, but when it came to Korbin she wanted to leave their past behind and just be there as a couple. Enjoying life, not worried about the next call or the next demon.

"Does it make me selfish to want that life more than the one where we help humanity?"

Korbin smiled. "Yeah, but that doesn't make it wrong. You are only human—"

"Half!" Stephanie pointed out.

"Yes, but the part that matters the most—that feels and dreams—is the human part. That is the part that is allowed to be selfish."

"Isn't that the only part that really matters?"

"Yeah, which means you should never feel bad about wanting those things."

"Who knows?" She sighed, putting her hands in her lap and looking around the complex. "Maybe one day we *will* be able to have those things. We might be too old to enjoy them, and we might be racing each other in motorized wheelchairs, but maybe we will see it in our lifetime."

"Those things are the dreams that keep me focused and fighting," Korbin admitted. "I think it's always been one of my motivations in this fight, but I didn't realize it until you came into my life. Thank you for that—for giving me yet another beautiful reason to keep on fighting. Every day I survive is another day closer to that perfect life. If not for me, then for the rest of humanity, and maybe even some people I know."

"It will be you." Stephanie nodded. "I feel it in my gut."

"You do?" Korbin chuckled and stood up, then reached down. "I think we should dance to that."

Stephanie puckered her lips, the corners of her mouth folding into a grin as she took his hand and let him pull her close. There was no music, but they didn't need it. The sound of breeze, the rustling of the sand, and the sparkling of the stars was the perfect orchestra for them. Korbin put one arm around her waist and held her hand close to his chest. He stared down into her eyes and she stared back, shaking her head in disbelief at how she had even gotten to where she was.

Korbin leaned down and kissed Stephanie's lips softly before bending his knees and picking her up, her hand still in his. She laughed as he whirled her around the impromptu dancefloor with their foreheads pressed together.

"I want you to do something for me," Korbin began, looking into her eyes.

"What's that?"

"If anything should ever happen to me..."

"No." She shook her head.

"Listen, if anything should happen, I want you to go. Get out of here and find that house with that garden and live your life. Don't stay and fight to the death after I am gone. The best tribute to my life would be for you to have one. A beautiful one with roses and lavender..."

"And a dog at my feet."

"Yep, a dog right there at your feet. Will you promise me that?"

Stephanie sighed and leaned into him.

"I promise."

5

B rock rolled up his sleeves and bent over to lift a heavy piece of wood into the back of his mother's truck. He should have known better than to think he would come home and not be put to work in one way or another.

He knew it was good for him, and with all the girls randomly snapping photos as they walked by it would be good for his persona too. They wouldn't think that he had gotten too big for his britches, even though he knew he had. He didn't care in the least.

"You need some help with that, man?" A tall, muscular guy with messy brown hair offered, picking up the other end of the wooden beam.

"Thanks, man," Brock told him. "Gotta make Mom happy."

"That's the only way," the guy responded. He had perfect dimples and a perfect smile. His teeth glistened like a toothpaste commercial, and something tingled deep inside Brock. He hadn't noticed it at first, but when his palms began to sweat he did.

Brock shook his head, realizing he had been staring a bit too long as they lifted the rest of the wood into the truck. He shook the guy's hand. "Brock."

"Erin," he responded. "You're the local superstar, right?"

"I guess you could say that." He chuckled, feeling his cheeks burn. "Just on vacation back home before we go on tour again. The road can get kind of crazy, so I wanted to check on the family and get back to my roots for a little while."

"Right." Erin nodded, noticing Brock was avoiding eye contact. "Well, if you need any more help let me know. I work just up the street and can always use a break."

"Will do. Thanks again."

Erin walked off and Brock leaned against the truck, his eyes glued to the guy's ass. It was perfect, as if he did squats at least once a day.

Suddenly he jumped, rubbed his hands over his face, and growled. He kicked a tire and grabbed his keys, getting into in the truck and laying his head down on the steering wheel. He slapped his hands against the side of his head.

"Get it together, motherfucker! That dude has a dick. You like girls, remember?"

Oh, relax, his succubus purred, her voice was soft. *He isn't your type anyway.*

Brock grunted. *Boys aren't my type in general.*

For now. The real reason is that he's too small; didn't even fill him out. Though I have to say those were some sweet lips. I bet he could use that mouth to compensate.

Ugh. Brock pulled his hands through his hair and

started the truck, turning the radio up to drown out the voice in his head. *Stop, okay? Just let me get this shit done without making me want to fucking throw up all over the place.*

So emotional! And they say women are the dramatic ones.

Brock drove back to his mom's house, which was right outside of town. It was an old two-story farmhouse with a wraparound porch that needed some love. He had gone to buy support beams and some new wood for the floor, thinking the drive would clear his mind.

The demon was too much for him. Too much stress, too much drama, and waaayyy too much *man-loving.*

Of course, *any* man-loving to Brock was too much.

He was a womanizer—always had been—and having a succubus inside him was damned confusing. He had never had a thought about a man in his whole life, even during some of his crazy nights with all kinds of naked bodies writhing around him.

He liked women, period fucking dot. In fact, lots and lots of fucking and dots.

And this damned demon was trying to *change* him.

When he got out of the truck his mom was standing on the porch wiping her hands on her apron and smiling. He climbed the stairs and kissed her on the cheek, trying to hide the turmoil that was bubbling inside.

"Sweetie, I need a favor."

"What's up, Momma?"

"Joann, who owns that little bar on the edge of town— she really needs a boost and her live music called sick tonight. I was wondering if you wouldn't play a set with the house band; stir up some of the locals to spend some money and help her out?"

Hot men! Woohoo!

Brock ignored the demon and smiled as he rubbed his mom's back gently. "Of course I will, Momma. No problem."

"You are the best." She smiled back and kissed him on the cheek. "I'll go call her and let her know."

His mother ran back into the house, and he caught the smell of dinner cooking on the stove as the door closed behind her. Brock sighed and sat down on the porch swing, then rocked back and forth. He had spent many nights in that porch swing, staring at the open fields and wondering if he would ever get out of that town. But after so many months on the road, it was *nice* to be home.

The only thing he couldn't seem to run from was the voice constantly chattering in his head.

It's been too long. I need one really sexy, hot man to just throw me down and go crazy.

You are driving me fucking nuts. *Is that all you think about? Sex, sex, and more sex?*

Pfft. *You're one to talk.*

Brock paused, stopping the swing and thinking about it for a moment.

His succubus had a point. He *was* being a bit of a hypocrite.

He had spent the last nine months with three women a night every night he could and twice a night one time, fulfilling his every desire. He thought about sex before his shows and during his shows, and even about how much sex he could get later after he was done having sex.

Yes, but, he yelled in his head. *I'm a guy! Look up guys in the dictionary and you'll find a picture of a horny male. That's just how we're built. We're supposed to chase tail and think about sex all the time.*

I think you underestimate the female mind, the succubus giggled. *What do you think those groupies are thinking while they are standing to the side of the stage applying their fourth layer of lip gloss, hiking up their skirts, and counting the condoms in their purses? Puppies? No. Dick, that's what they are thinking about.*

Brock shook his head and leaned back on the swing, realizing that there *was* a bit of a double standard going on —and he was the one perpetrating it. For some reason he couldn't understand why it was okay for him to be a slut, to think about getting some all the time, talk about it, and do it even, but he was upset because his succubus couldn't get past it.

She was really the same as him, only with a different sexual preference.

His eyes opened wide when he realized he'd not only had met the female version of himself, but she was literally inside his body, pushing desires on him and acting just like he did on a normal basis.

Every day he woke up thinking about sex, only the thoughts were about being with men—and he could tell from his man stuff the demon was messing with his body. There was no way he would get that reaction on his own. Maybe he should have taken his mother's advice and stayed in town to work at the mill like everyone else, but nooooo—he had to be a rock star!

He rubbed his eyes. "Talk about fucking karma," he mumbled.

Joshua smiled as he looked down at his clipboard, checking off the massive amounts of ammo being pumped out in the manufacturing area they had built. He couldn't believe they had gotten it together so quickly and were now pretty much working at full capacity. His equation and ideas had worked, and because of Katie and the team, they were a *real* business. His father would have been proud of him —*that* he knew for sure.

Charles and Travis grunted as they picked up the metal ammo containers and stacked them in the back. The boxes were full to the top and bore a black-stamped label designating what type of round they were and letting the troops know they were special and possibly even toxic.

The team hadn't come into the factory much since they had started using chemicals that had the ability to cause them excruciating pain.

The girls had moved from their normal duties into racking and stacking with the guys. The military was not slowing down their orders, so they needed as much help as they could get. Even with the seven guys the general had sent over, there was more than enough work. Overtime had become the norm, and the schedule had shifted to twenty-four-hour days for the military guys. One day on, twelve hours off, six days a week. No one complained though, especially after they were briefed on the situation.

"How's it going?"

Joshua looked at one of the older guys from the general's group and shook his head. "It's crazy. I would have never believed we could produce this kind of ammo in such high volumes, and from the tests, it doesn't look like it's lost any of its integrity. We originally thought sixty thousand rounds by the end of the week, but it's looking more like eighty thousand if we keep this up."

"That's good. Telling those boys in the field to only shoot minimal rounds sounds good in theory, but if you have one of those creatures barreling down on you then you're not taking the time to count out how many times you've pulled that trigger. You just want them dead."

"Oh, I understand." Joshua chuckled nervously. "I killed one with a knife once. Would have been nice to have something a little more removed. I definitely wouldn't have been counting bullets, though."

The soldier lifted an eyebrow. "You've seen combat?"

He pointed around the building. "Me and every single one of these girls." Joshua nodded at the group, who were smiling and talking while they loaded the rounds into their boxes.

"You'd think that after everything I've seen nothing would surprise me anymore. Well, good job. We need more good people like that out here. I never thought I'd face a threat like this when I signed up. Definitely another one on the list of things my recruiter didn't mention." He patted Joshua on the shoulder.

Joshua took a deep breath. He wasn't quite used to being so close to other people, especially strangers, but he was doing better than he used to.

He put the pen in the latch on the clipboard and stared across the factory floor. They had created some new weapons that the military had put in an order for to test during their next big mission. That area was completely off limits to any of the Damned, since it was highly dangerous to them.

"When will we send out the next shipment?"

Joshua shook his away thoughts and looked down at the clipboard. "It looks like we will have a shipment ready to air-ship out of here tomorrow. The military is keeping us busy; ordered a *shit-ton* of metal from us. We'll probably continue producing and shipping like this until the war is over or until we come up with something even bigger and more badass, which happens on the regular around here."

"Yeah? Next thing I know you'll be producing warheads."

"If we could bomb hell, you know we would." Joshua laughed, setting down his clipboard and looking at the guy. "Come with me and I'll show you some of the new stuff." Joshua stopped and turned back to the soldier. "You're not Damned, are you?"

He chuckled. "Me? No. Though it doesn't seem like that bad a choice when I watch your friends out there kicking ass."

Joshua shrugged. "Yeah, well, I'm good not sharing my body with anything."

Joshua walked the contact to the restricted area of the floor, which was where all the new products were made. It was the most volatile, and at high risk for spillage. Joshua grabbed two pairs of metalworking gloves and handed a pair to the soldier before pulling his on.

"You can never be too cautious," Joshua told him

"What's all this?" the military liaison asked, pulling on his gloves.

"The general was looking for big guns, the stuff that

would do some serious damage to the demons and make for fewer casualties among his troops. We started to do some research, looking into what weapons existed and how we could modify them."

Joshua picked up one of their 30mm fragmentation rounds. "This sucker is made of the metals, and inside is not only an explosive, but it launches slivers of this outward. You could shoot one of these into a crowd of demons or one big-ass motherfucker and it would send little ones through his whole body."

"Damn."

Joshua picked up a teargas round. "This looks like a normal teargas round, right?"

"Yeah."

"It's not. We ground the special metal to dust and put it in the teargas round. The human hosts are affected by the tear gas and it disables the physical body, while the metal dust gets into the demon through the lungs. You are taking down two with one shot, and it's not lethal in small doses —so if we want to capture some of them for testing we can. Otherwise, we are disabling them enough to get in and take them out."

"Shit, that's brilliant!"

Joshua nodded. "We are currently working on grenades made from the metal, and possibly teargas grenades, depending on what the military wants. This teargas mixture could be pertinent in many different scenarios, including when there is a demon causing mass panic. If you use it there, you are going to find demons on the ground unable to move. Of course, we haven't yet tested the harm the metal dust will do to a normal human, but the military doesn't seem to be too concerned."

"Shoot first, ask questions later." The soldier chuckled. "As long as it takes down the enemy they are willing to figure out the rest later. In this situation, I don't much blame them: you either die from the demon or take your chances with the tear gas. I'd choose the teargas any time."

"Most people who have seen one of these things in action would."

They put the rounds back and took off the gloves as they made their way to the front. Things in the manufactory were working like a well-oiled machine. The soldier shook his head, still computing everything he had been briefed on when he had been assigned to work there. He looked at Joshua, thinking about how meek and fragile he appeared on the outside. It was obvious he had the heart of a warrior.

The liaison nodded to the machines. "Let me ask you something... How did you get into this business?"

Joshua smiled. "It's a family thing."

6

General Brushwood had received notification that a huge shipment of ammo would be sent out the next day. Things were quiet on the home front, and though that normally would be considered a good thing, it made him nervous. The sonsabitches were planning something; he could feel it in his bones.

He had been serving long enough to have developed that kind of intuition, just like when he had been in the war. This was the calm before the storm, and it made him a little more than anxious.

A voice came over the intercom. "General, Colonel Jehovivich is here to see you, sir."

"Send her in," he replied.

The door to his office opened and the colonel came in and stood at attention. The general waved her in and she approached the desk. She set a file on his desk and handed him a flash drive.

"It's the after-action report. We thought you would like

to take it in here instead of the comm room. The file has everything you have already seen, and the thumb drive is the video footage from the chest cameras and those mounted on the helicopters."

"Not that I am chomping at the bit to see this battle, but something about it has been gnawing at my gut since I was given the briefs."

The general pushed back from his desk and turned his monitor so the colonel could watch with him, then put the thumb drive into his computer and clicked on the file. They had compiled the footage for him, one camera fading into another to show the situation from different angles. The beginning showed the soldiers crouched in the greenery. The video progressed, pausing as the first body came into view.

Jehovivich pointed at the screen. "That was one of the demons Katie killed."

"Jesus." The general leaned forward to get a closer view. "They are barely adults."

"With all due respect, sir, I don't think the demons have a moral code…and we send out men just as young."

"True." The general waved his finger at the colonel. "Good way of keeping it in perspective."

The colonel pressed the forward button. "So this is where Katie and Damian walk into the hotel."

The general squinted at Katie's back. She looked different somehow; taller and curvier than he had remembered. He just figured it was the footage and his aging eyes.

"So this is where Katie and Damian are fighting demons inside. You will see a couple attempted escapes, but it doesn't escalate until…here."

The colonel pressed Play again to resume normal speed and they watched the last gruesome scene of the fight. The general sighed, shaking his head and leaning back in his chair.

"Just as they described it. I've seen men die in war, but it never gets easier to watch, even on a television screen."

"Wait," the colonel exclaimed, narrowing her eyes. "Rewind that... Stop! Press play."

The video on the screen was from one of the choppers, which was swooping around the scene after the portal had closed. The helicopter moved along the front of the hotel, getting ready to land. Jehovivich pressed the Enter key.

"Stop. There...in the window. Is that Katie?"

The general lifted his glasses and moved closer to the screen, squinting at the face in the window. It definitely wasn't Katie, and she looked *pissed*.

Jehovivich spoke again. "That's *not* Katie, and whoever it is, they are annoyed at the people below."

"Or annoyed they got away," the general added.

"But her eyes—they are glowing, so she is obviously a demon."

The general nodded, pressing Play again and watching until the woman moved out of sight. It was strange—she looked similar enough to be mistaken for Katie, but it definitely *wasn't* her.

Jehovivich picked up the phone and started to dial. "I'll put out an APB on this character."

"Wait." The general grabbed her hand and she looked at him in confusion, then slowly lowered the handset.

"I need to get more intel on this. Fire up my chopper."

"But sir, there could be a risk!"

"My helicopter, please," the general repeated.

Jehovivich stopped arguing and left the room to prepare for the general's departure. Brushwood returned to his computer and played the video clip over and over in a bid to figure out the identity of the woman in the window.

Whoever she was, he had a feeling the mercenaries *weren't* in the dark.

Korbin walked into his office with a smile on his face, just having finished lunch with Stephanie. She had put together some egg salad sandwiches and they had attempted to eat outside, but the wind was heavy that day and all he got to eat were mouthfuls of sand.

They ended up eating in the conference room for a bit of privacy. He couldn't believe that amongst all the turmoil and trials he had found the woman he loved—and that this relationship was actually working, for once.

He turned to his computer and pulled up a whole new set of emails. He sighed and began to click through them, responding when appropriate. He wasn't used to things being so calm. Office work felt like drudgery. He was almost bored enough to wish for a call, but since the hotel situation there had been none.

While Korbin was straightening the papers on his desk the phone rang, and a tingle of adrenaline hit him in the chest. He knew that the phone didn't ring for social calls anymore. He picked it up eagerly.

"This is Korbin."

"Hey, this is Sergeant Alvis from the Las Vegas PD. We have a terrorist situation in progress, and I was told to call you and ask for assistance."

"What kind of situation?" Korbin's heart started to beat faster.

"We have multiple hostages, and what you might call 'abnormal perpetrators.'"

"Location?"

Korbin wrote it down, along with the limited details they had. It had been a while since they had gotten a hometown call, but that was what the team needed—to keep going and not get too lost in the downtime.

"We'll be there as soon as possible," Korbin told him, then hung up.

He pushed back from his desk and looked around the quiet room for a moment, gathering his thoughts. There was something in the air; he could feel it. He didn't *think* it was this call, although he couldn't be sure. Finally! He slapped the button on his desk to send off the alert.

It's go time!

Katie put her hands on her knees and breathed heavily as she tried to control her laughter. Calvin groaned and rolled over on the mat, pushing up on his big arms to lift himself to his feet. He shook his head, wiping the sweat from his forehead with the bottom of his shirt.

"You're getting back to your old self again." Katie smirked. "I was wondering how long it would take for you to be back at full strength after that hit in the cemetery."

"Hey, I'm just tired, that's all. I'm back, and better than ever."

"Sometimes when we start to age... Well, no one's blaming you, dude."

Calvin snickered and lowered himself into a defensive stance. "All right, you got jokes. Come at me, then. I'll show you how this old man rocks and rolls."

Katie chuckled. "More like creaks and rattles."

Calvin shook his head and lunged at her, swiping his hand at her face. She swayed just out of his reach, nodding as she bounced on her toes. "Oh-ho! Getting wily, are we? Better slow down, old man. You might break a hip."

Calvin ran forward and grabbed Katie around the waist, then lifted her into the air. She laughed and shrugged at Eric's catcall from the sidelines, then wrapped her legs around Calvin's waist and put her hands on his shoulders.

All right, give me a boost.

I don't know. I kind of like this.

Pandora!

Fine.

Pandora juiced Katie and she jumped upward, balancing on his shoulders for a moment before jumping to the floor behind him. Before he could turn around she swung a low leg at his ankles, knocking him to the ground. He laid there face-down, breathing heavily and laughing.

"I swear, one of these days you are gonna break one of us, Pandora. And don't act surprised. I know Katie doesn't have that kind of agility."

Eric laughed. "Cheater."

"You only think that way when you are on the losing

team," Katie told him, shaking her head. "Otherwise you are all about playing dirty."

I'm always *about playing dirty.* Pandora sighed. *But alas, no lovers to be found.*

Shhh.

Katie offered Calvin a hand up and they stood together for a moment, panting and still chuckling. Eric tossed them bottles of water and towels, then leaned back against the edge of the matted area and shook his head.

"One of these days you are gonna wear yourselves out like that, then—"

Just then the alarm went off overhead, startling Eric. His mouth dropped open and he pointed up at the speaker.

"It's like it can *read my damned mind.*"

Katie chuckled and headed to the bench to pull on her boots. Korbin's voice crackled over the loudspeaker.

"Calvin, Eric, Katie, and Stephanie, please come to the conference room. We have a call."

Calvin grabbed his bag out of the locker. "I feel like the Ghostbusters."

"We just need the firemen's pole." Eric smirked.

"I don't trust Pandora around a shiny silver pole to save my life." Katie grimaced.

Calvin spoke up. "I kind of like the sound of that."

Katie swatted Calvin with her towel as the three headed out of the training area, meeting up with Stephanie in the hallway. She looked at their sweaty bodies and smiled.

"Katie call you old again?"

Katie laughed. "You mean, did I tell him the cold, hard truth?"

She massaged Calvin's shoulders as they entered the

conference room in high spirits. However, as soon as they hit the door and saw the look on Korbin's face they settled down. Katie hadn't seen him that serious in a long time, which either meant this call was big or something big was coming.

Either way, it was setting up to be a hell of a day.

Katie took a seat next to Stephanie and folded her hands in front of her. She looked across the table at Calvin and Eric who had their eyes locked on Korbin. Korbin shuffled his papers on his desk and sighed.

"We have a call from the Las Vegas Police Department. There are limited details, but we know there are hostages and a large group of what they are calling terrorists and 'abnormal perpetrators.' They believe something odd is happening, so they found it best to call us. I think we are looking at a decent-sized incursion."

"Okay." Calvin put his hands down to stand up.

Korbin put up a hand. "Hold on. I have a gut feeling there is more going on—maybe not with this, but somewhere else. I want you to stay alert and ready, just in case you have to bounce from one incursion to another."

Calvin gave him a salute, Eric nodded in understanding, and Stephanie reached out to grip his arm with a kind smile. Katie could see the energy they shared; Stephanie had really become a calming influence in Korbin's life.

Katie liked that, and Korbin deserved it, especially after all the sacrifices he had made for the team and the cause. A little bit of happiness in the between-times; everyone needed that.

She nodded. "Sounds good, boss."

She could tell he was on edge, but she needed to focus

on the job at hand. They got up and left the rocm, heading toward the training center to retrieve their weapons. Katie grabbed two pistols and put them in their holsters on her waist, then looked around at the other weapons. She wasn't sure she would need anything else. If it was that bad she could release Pandora, and if not she would just kick their asses like normal. She hated being weighed down by gear.

Take your staff, Pandora ordered.

Are you sure?

You're ready.

Katie shrugged and pulled her staff out of the cabinet, sliding it carefully into her back strap. She had practiced with it quite a bit, and if Pandora thought she was ready she wouldn't let her fail.

Katie walked back out to the lockers and pulled her hair back into a tight ponytail while she waited for the others to finish zipping their bags.

"Hey, bitches. Looky what I got?" Stephanie sang out, dangling a key. "I'll be your pilot this evening. Please keep your tray tables in their locked and upright position."

"Uh..." Calvin lifted an eyebrow.

"I've been learning how to fly the beast while you slackers were out eating donuts. Come on, let's hit the road."

She left the room and Katie shook her head, then put her bag over her shoulder and patted Eric and Calvin on their backs. As they all walked behind them toward the elevator she reminded them, "Hey, there are worse ways to die, especially in this profession."

Calvin scoffed. "That's definitely true but it doesn't

make me feel any better about jumping into the chopper with Rambette."

Eric put his arm around Calvin. "Think of it this way: you'll die at the hand of a beautiful woman. And besides, Pandora has got this. She'll save your tender little body."

Damn right, big man, Pandora shouted. *Then we'll* really *see what you're made of.*

Calvin looked at Katie, who was grimacing. "She said something, didn't she?"

Katie winked at him. "Doesn't she always?"

The team smiled as they left the elevator and headed to the helo pad, covering their eyes from the blowing sand. They climbed into the chopper and put on their headsets, then peered at Stephanie—who was just sitting there staring at the controls. Calvin looked at Eric and back at their pilot.

"Everything all right, Stephanie?"

"Yeah, I just can't remember how to turn the thing on."

Eric buckled his belt. "We're all gonna die."

"Ha! Just fuckin' with ya. Sit back and enjoy the ride, pussies. I swear, men are all He-Man—until they're not."

"Preach it, sister," Pandora barked from Katie's throat.

Eric and Calvin looked up and Katie just shrugged, giving Stephanie a wink. It was nice heading to these things with family. It took the edge off to know that if they were in trouble one of them would be there.

7

B rock stood in the band room at the back of the bar.
He was amused that the owner wanted to announce him as a surprise. He looked at the original poster for that night's entertainment and chuckled. The band did covers of his music. *His* band was called "The Straights" and the cover band was called "The Curves."

Interesting that they already had kids riding their coattails.

At least the audience would know the music, and hopefully the house band would too. Otherwise it would be a shitty show. Still, it was probably the biggest thing the small town had seen since the seventies. There was a knock on the door and a huge bald bouncer stuck his head in.

"Ready in five."

Brock studied the guy's face; there was something familiar about him. "Hey, didn't we go to school together?"

The bouncer smiled and stuck out his hand. "Yeah, high school."

"Good to see you, man."

"You too," the bouncer replied, looking curiously at Brock's eyes as a flash of red moved across them. "Cool contacts, dude."

Brock glanced in the mirror, then realized what he was talking about and blinked wildly. "Thanks. You know, gotta bring something special."

"I hear ya." He laughed and shut the door.

Come on, stop putting on a show, Brock growled.

That guy was beefcake. A little too big for my taste, but hey, I'm in a drought.

"Shut up," Brock yelled out loud just as the door opened.

"Practicing for tonight?" the manager asked, raising an eyebrow.

Brock patted his neck. "Oh, yeah, you know, warming up the vocal cords."

"Good, 'cause it's time. We'll go up on the stage, you stand in the shadow, and I'll get you introduced."

"Sounds good." Brock got up from his chair.

He grabbed his guitar and followed her onto the stage, where he stood out of the lights while he plugged his guitar into the amp.

A bright spotlight hit the stage, showing the manager to the crowd. The bar was medium-sized and packed with people wearing a mixture of his band's shirt and the other band's gear. She cleared her throat and tapped the mic to make sure it was on.

"Everybody having a good time?" The crowd cheered.

"Good, cause it's about to get a *hell* of a lot better. The Curves were unable to show up tonight for personal reasons, but..."

The crowd booed. She shook her head and put her hand in the air.

"*But* I have something even *better*. On break from their tour and performing tonight with our house band is The Straights' very own...Brock Rutherford!"

The crowd cheered as Brock walked into the spotlight with his hands in the air. Immediately the band started playing, rolling right into their first song. Brock was surprised by how easily it came, even though he was in vacation mode. Even his demon was quiet at first, which never happened these days.

"Take it to the brink..." he sang, the crowd singing along with him. "Show 'em who comes first. Take it to the brink..."

Take it to my thang... the demon sang in his head. *Give it to me all night long. Take it to my thang...*

Good lord, that's terrible. Brock grumbled.

He kept a smile on his face and his lyrics straight, determined not to show how difficult it was to perform with a demon singing different lyrics in his head. The song ended and the crowd cheered, which didn't drown out the sound of his succubus cackling. He launched right into the next one, a slower ballad. The one all the ladies loved.

"Beautiful girl..." he sang. "Like roses in the springtime, my love for you will never fade away."

Beautiful boy... the succubus repeated. *Like the crevasse of your abdomen, my tongue will never fade. Beautiful boy...*

That's really getting annoying.

Look at all those boys! They are just dying *to get a piece of me.*

I really doubt that. Most of these guys only want to get close to me to get close to the girls.

What about that hot piece of meat right there in the front? I'd get him naked so fast he wouldn't even know what hit him.

Brock sang louder, scanning the front row to find the target his demon had homed in on. He grimaced, shaking his head for a moment but then stopping himself.

He needed to figure out how to control this bitch, because shit had just gone *too* far.

Oh my God, you are talking about Eric Schism! That guy barely made it out of high school.

Like I care? His package is huge! *His brain could be the size of my pinky for all I care, as long as he can get it up.*

That's fucking disgusting.

No, what was disgusting was that brunette you banged back in St. Louis—the one with the weird obsession with My Little Pony. *This guy has all the qualifications to roll right into my panties. Perfect muscular chest, arms the size of your head, and holy* shit *he has the V.*

What the hell is "the V?"

Those muscles, you know? The ones that run down his abdomen like an arrow right to the good stuff. You just put your mouth there and follow the yellow brick road.

The song ended and he shivered, feeling almost nauseous thinking about Eric's V—or anything else that had to do with a naked Eric.

Are all *chicks like this, or just you? Because* you *are like a hyper-driven sexual predator.*

Shit, get girls alone with a bottle or six of wine and you will hear things that will make you want to wash your brain. The dick might not be so pretty, but everything leading up to it is. And no one gives a shit if it's pretty as long as it goes in and does the job.

I thought size really didn't matter?

Bullshit! Girls only say that when their man has a small one so they don't feel so bad. Given the choice, poof—*nine inches of sexual prowess at your door.*

Not at my fucking door.

You will come around. I promise."

Brock shook it off, finishing the song and taking a break. At the bar he ordered a shot of Jameson and a beer, throwing back the shot and taking a gulp of the beer.

That's right, get wasted. So much easier to control you when you're blacked-out drunk.

Brock turned and spat out the beer, almost spraying a group of fans behind him. They giggled as he slammed the beer on the bar and took a deep breath before he reached for their pens to sign whatever they had, including the shirts on their bodies. He tried to smile, but the irritation was building inside him.

He couldn't even have a drink at his own damn show without this bitch trying to ruin it for him. He didn't know what he was going to do, but he had to give her *something* to shut her up.

He finished signing autographs and walked over to Eric, who was leaning against the stage and typing on his phone. Brock took a deep breath and plastered a smile on his face.

"Eric, man, it's good to see you. It's been forever!"

Eric's eyebrows shot up. "Hey, I didn't think you would remember me."

Oh shit, oh shit! Shake his hand. Let me feel it.

Brock gritted his teeth and held out a hand for a firm shake, patting the back of Eric's hand with the other. He had to admit, with the succubus controlling his every move and half his libido, Eric wasn't that bad looking a guy.

He pulled his hand back and shoved it in his pocket, immediately regretting the thought.

Brock kept the smile going. "What have you been up to?"

"I own a mechanic shop on the east side of town. You know, next to Greene's Grocery?"

"Oh, nice! I'll have to let my ma know so when she gets work done she'll come see you."

"She actually already does. She's a real nice lady. Brings me cookies and stuff when she comes in."

"Ha, sounds like my mom."

Make plans with him, his succubus hissed. *Do it. Do it and I'll shut up for the rest of the night.*

And you won't fuck with me when I get drunk?

She didn't hesitate. *Deal.*

Brock took a deep breath and looked at the stage. "I gotta get back onstage, but why don't we catch up? We could grab some wings and beers from Farley's or something."

Eric grinned and nodded enthusiastically. "Yeah, man! When's good?"

"Uh, how about Friday?"

"Cool. Just come on over to the shop. We close at six on Fridays."

"Sounds good."

Brock nodded and headed back to the stage, where he picked up his guitar.

Not a peep from his succubus. He had *finally* won one fucking moment of quiet.

It was going to be a long existence if he had to keep bribing her like that, but all he cared about was getting through the night.

———

The chopper landed just outside the cordoned-off building in a cement courtyard of sorts. The place looked rundown, but it still had electricity so it wasn't abandoned. Katie, Calvin, Eric, and Stephanie waited for the helicopter blades to slow, then piled out and headed over to the group of cops gathered behind two large barriers.

The captain looked up, elbowing his sergeant as the four approached.

"Looks like the D squad is here."

The sergeant sighed. "Finally! I was starting to think blowing the place was an option."

Katie walked up first, hand out. "Captain, we are here from—"

"We know, the D squad," he replied, shaking her hand.

Katie chuckled and introduced the others. "Yeah, the D squad. I'm Katie, this is Calvin, Eric, and Stephanie. How many men have you got inside the building?"

"Inside?" He shook his head. "None. We can't even get a foot through the door without some crazed red-eyed freak running us off."

"All right, that's probably for the best." Katie looked down at the map in front of the captain. "What do we know?"

"Well, here on the first floor we got about ten terrorists holding upward of fifteen hostages, and then up here on the eighth floor, ten more terrorists with about the same number of hostages. We tried to talk to them, but there is nothing but growling and some language I don't understand."

Calvin shook his head. "Demons. Can't communicate worth shit."

The captain raised an eyebrow, but he had heard the stories. He knew the precinct hadn't been told the whole truth about some of the crazy crime going on in Vegas, but he hadn't thought he would ever be called to a scene where there were actual *demons*.

He was getting too old for this shit, and had seen too much to start adding creatures from another plane to his list.

"We will back you," the captain told Katie. "Just tell us how many men to send in with you."

"None." Katie looked down to make sure her pistols were loaded.

"None? There are twenty or more terrorists in there with gleaming red eyes."

"I know. And four badass Damned right here, ready to rip their throats out." Katie smiled and patted the captain on the shoulder. "Is this your first demon experience?"

He pursed his lips. "If we don't count my two ex-wives, yes."

Katie provided the appropriate laugh to release his

anxiety. "It's all right. Just keep your men surrounding the building. Anyone who's not a hostage or anyone with red eyes who *isn't* one of us gets a bullet straight to the head. No playing around. You don't want any of these bastards ending up out in the streets. They may look kind of like people, but I promise you they aren't. Not anymore. The person they were is gone. It's just a demon wearing their skin. There are two types of infected: those who control their demon and those who are controlled and used for their bodies. These are the *controlled*."

Katie went to leave but stopped and looked at the captain.

"And don't be surprised if you kill one and they turn to dust."

"Dust?" The captain sighed and nodded, getting on his walkie-talkie. "All forces, stand down. Do not fire unless told to. Surround the building. We have a specialty force of...four going in to handle this. Over."

"I'm sorry, Captain, it sounded like you said *four*? Over."

"I did. They're from the D squad."

Katie pulled Calvin, Eric, and Stephanie into a huddle. Calvin rubbed his hands together and looked up at the building, obviously ready for some action. The whole crew had just stood by while Katie and Damian had taken on the demons in the hotel, but this time they got to stretch their legs a bit. Katie was always on the line those days, and she could only imagine the frustration of sitting on the sidelines waiting for her turn to kick some ass.

After all, it was their entire purpose in life. It wasn't like there was much else to do.

"What we got?"

Katie nodded. "We got twenty demons split between the first and eighth floor. We got twenty or more hostages as well. We don't know if anyone is injured or dead at this point. Calvin, you, Eric, and Stephanie take the first floor, and I'll take the eighth."

"By yourself?"

Katie just gave him a look and smirked. "You guys got the right ammo?"

Stephanie and Eric nodded and Calvin double-checked his weapons. Katie looked up at the building, scanning from the first floor up to the eighth. She wondered what she would be facing up there. Lower-level? Huge? T'Chezz, even? After the last few days, she was ready for just about anything.

Katie put her hand to her mouth and coughed to clear her throat, then rubbed her hand across her chest. She felt a burning sensation like acid reflux, but she'd never had that issue before and she hadn't eaten anything for hours. Calvin eyed her suspiciously as he holstered his weapons, then put his hand on her shoulder.

"You all right?"

Katie waved him off. "Yeah, it's just... You know what? It's nothing. Let's kick some ass."

"You need some back... No, wait—I know the answer to this one. You carry your backup."

Pandora's voice echoed from Katie's throat. "Damn right she does."

The captain jumped slightly, eyeing Katie fearfully. Calvin laughed and shrugged.

Katie headed toward the building with the strange

feeling in her chest at the front of her mind. *What the hell was that?*

You felt the demons, Pandora answered.

What?

That burning—that was you feeling out the demons. It was light, like heartburn, meaning there's nothing too daunting up there. Figured I would let you feel it before you asked about what you were facing.

Well, isn't that nifty? You ready to kick some ass?

Always.

8

The team entered into the side stairwell and faced the first-floor doors. Katie paused on the first step and looked back at them, feeling that burning sensation again.

"They're low-level, but there are a lot of them. Keep your eyes open and don't walk into anything blindly."

All three nodded and pulled their weapons. Stephanie stepped to the door and took the handle, looking up at Katie. Katie made her way up the stairs two at a time, getting to the eighth floor a lot faster than she had expected.

She paused to listen to the gunfire below, hoping they all left in one piece, then put her hand on the door and closed her eyes to sense the energy in the hallway. She flung the door open and pulled both pistols, keeping her right one raised as she cleared each room.

She knew they were in there somewhere, but she could only assume they had sensed Pandora and moved back for a major attack.

At the end of the hall were two double doors with an old sign posted above that read, The Hancock Ballroom. The room would be large, but in an old building like this there wouldn't be many hiding places.

Carefully she grabbed the handle, twisting it until it clicked, and kicked the door open, holding both pistols in the air.

There were ten hostages bound together in the center of the room. They made noises through their gags and their eyes darted all over the place. A balding man in the front stared at her with sweat running down his forehead. Suddenly his eyes flashed behind her. She turned as a demon jumped from its perch above the doorway and pulled the trigger on her Glock, hammering four rounds straight into his chest.

The demon screamed in a high pitch as the special metal of her bullets incapacitated him. She walked up and pointed the gun at his head; his eyes were glowing red and there was blood trickling from his mouth. She smiled and pulled the trigger again, and the demon was dust before the blood splatter from the shot hit the old wooden doors behind him.

Immediately other demons began to attack from all sides. Katie spun, unloading the last ten bullets in her gun as she turned. She holstered her empty weapon and tossed the one in her left hand to her right. She counted the piles of dust; she'd only killed three so far.

That meant there were still seven lurking in the shadows.

She carefully stepped forward and her boot crunched

on a broken shard of glass. Behind her, she could hear the rapid breathing of another demon.

She spun around with a twist of her hips to shove the demon back, then shot him three times in the chest. The fourth bullet shattered his skull. The burning sensation in her chest raged as the fifth and sixth demons ran toward her slashing their claws. She unloaded the rest of the clip in their direction, mostly hitting the demons' legs and arms. She holstered her gun and cracked her knuckles as they writhed in pain on the floor, the metal poisoning their senses.

"I gotta work on my aim," she joked, pulling her staff from her back.

She twisted it apart and lowered the two halves to her sides, snapping the blades out. She smiled and walked slowly toward the injured demons, who were snapping their sharp teeth and scoring the floor with their claws. She whirled, raised both halves of her staff into the air, and slammed them into the demon's skulls. A loud hiss echoed through the room as they turned to dust.

She straightened up when she heard the tapping of claws behind her. The last four demons snarled at her as they came forward together, watching her closely as she turned with both staffs gripped firmly in her hands.

"*There* you are. I wondered when you were going to show up."

The largest of the demons, who was small compared to others she had faced, stepped forward. He barely had any recognizable human attributes. His black body was covered in scales, and his eyes shone brightly in the dim room.

Katie yawned and looked at the hostages. Several of them had passed out from sheer terror.

Use the kata I showed you.

"My demon—you know, the one you can sense?—has given me a heads-up. You don't know karate, but guess what?" Katie tapped the blade of her staff on the floor. "I do!"

She put herself in a defensive stance, raising both halves of her staff to her sides. She stepped forward and screamed as she sliced the poles through the air. She moved back and forth, putting on a show, swinging a staff and stopping an inch from the demon's head. She smirked at him for a moment.

The demon's red eyes glowed fearlessly back at her and he growled, swiping out at her as she did a backflip and landed solidly on her feet. She positioned one staff in front and one in back, then crouched.

The demon hissed and the others came running. They surrounded her, taking their moment in the sun to attack. She kicked forward, sending one tripping into another before jumping up and landing on its chest. She raised her poles and struck downward, finding his skull. He screamed his agony and turned to dust beneath her feet.

Another demon had run up from behind and now jumped Katie as she was finishing the other two, sinking his claw into her shoulder.

Katie straightened and flung her arms back, yelling her pain. The demon fell to the floor, but was only down for a second before he scrambled back to his feet and lunged for her chest with his sharp fangs.

Katie growled and her eyes glowed brightly as she

swung her staff to connect with his head in mid-air. He fell to the ground, taking the staff with him, and writhed for a moment before turning to dust. Before Katie could retrieve her staff the next demon was on her, trying for the same shoulder.

She whirled and brought her leg into the air to kick the demon in the neck. She threw down her other staff and jumped onto the demon's shoulders, then pushed her fingers into his red eyes. He screamed and thrashed wildly as the blood squirted from his eye sockets and she took her hands away, then grabbed his head and twisted to break his neck. The resulting dust fell almost unnoticed to the floor as she turned her attention to the last of the demons.

The largest one was sprinting for the window. She shook her head as she walked toward him, pausing only to pick up one of her half-staffs "Hey!"

The demon stopped and turned around, but took another step backward. He stared at her, his eyes darting to and fro as his fear overwhelmed him.

Katie shook her head, looking first at him and then at her sharp-bladed staff.

"You're nothing but a coward after all."

She took a step forward, flinging the staff blade-first like a spear. It hit him in the chest and sent him crashing back into the glass. His weight was too much and shattered the window, so Katie ran forward and grabbed the handle of her weapon to stop the demon from falling.

She was shaking her head. "Oh, *hell* no! You are *not* taking my fucking *staff* with you!"

She stamped a foot into the demon's stomach, pulling back on the staff embedded in the demon's chest to free it as the force of her kick propelled him out the window. She peered out to see the demon plummet toward the cement and a loud hopeless shriek came from his throat as he fell.

She nodded in satisfaction, as he turned to dust just before he hit the ground, where it plumed like a mini mushroom cloud. The ring of cops below were all watching with wide eyes and the captain stood at the front, shaking his head in disbelief.

Katie smiled and waved to the few cops looking up at the window, then went quickly to the hostages.

She crouched to untie the man in the front and pulled off his gag. He looked around the room in amazement, the sweat still shimmering on his bald scalp.

"You are safe here. Don't leave this room until we or the cops come and get you. There are others downstairs, and they need to be handled before it is safe for you to leave this room. Do you understand? I am making you the leader."

The man nodded and looked at the others as Katie stood up. "Good. Where the hell is the elevator in this place?"

Calvin, Stephanie, and Eric entered the first floor and moved carefully through the lobby. There was a large room to the right, an auditorium of some sort with peeling paint. The place had been left in disrepair. Stephanie stopped at the doors and motioned for the others to move forward. She pointed to Calvin and motioned to the left, then to Eric, motioning to the right.

She would go straight down the center.

They crept through the already-open doors into the pitch-black room. Calvin stayed low and moved to the left, Eric crept along the wall to the right, and Stephanie headed down the main row between the seating areas.

Suddenly a spotlight came on, illuminating the stage in front of them. The torn curtains on the sides rustled and the hostages sat bound together in the center, some of them injured and others just scared.

Seven demons slowly crept out onto the stage holding assault-style weapons.

"This is different," Calvin whispered. He was used to his team being the only ones with guns.

The demons lined up at the front of the stage with the hostages behind them and sprayed bullets into the seating areas, unable to see where the three crouched. Calvin pulled his rifle from his back and aimed over the backs of the chairs, letting out a deep breath as he shot the demon on the far end. The beast dropped his gun, jerked backward from the shot in his shoulder. He stood there for a moment before grabbing the injury with a long, high squeal. Calvin took aim again, this time shooting him right between the eyes. His body fell to dust and the other demons growled and jumped from the stage.

Eric, Stephanie, and Calvin returned fire, dodging in and out of the seats as they tried not to get hit by the bullets flying around the room. Eric stood next to the elevator doors and aimed toward the demons.

Two headshots, two more demons down.

The elevator doors dinged and Eric raised his gun when a demon rolled out with his weapon pointed toward Stephanie's back. Eric jumped into action, hooking his rifle around the demon's neck and pulling back tightly as the demon lashed back and forth, unable to draw breath due to the pressure of Eric's rifle against his windpipe.

Eric let go of his gun and pulled his knife in a lightning move, bringing it up to stab the demon in the chest. The demon let go of his gun and fell to his knees as Eric twisted the knife inside him.

Echoing screams filled the room, the metal putting any demon it touched out of commission. Eric removed the knife and dropped his rifle. The demon clawed at the large hole in his chest for several moments.

"Die already," Eric yelled, slashing its scaly black neck with the knife.

The demon dropped to the floor and turned to dust, leaving Eric on all fours trying to catch his breath. Stephanie looked at him and nodded in thanks, then her eyes grew wide and she whirled around, sending three shots into the air above Eric's head. Eric rose to his knees as a demon with bullet holes in his chest hit the ground right in front of him. He pulled the sword off his back and brought it down hard to sever the demon's head.

"Watch out," Calvin yelled to Stephanie, and she turned just in time to catch the demon as it fell toward her. Her gun slid across the floor as she wrestled with it and they rolled through the open walkway between the seats, the demon coming out on top as they ground to a stop. Stephanie almost gagged at its rancid breath as he growled and hissed at her. She gripped his throat to keep him from sinking his teeth into her.

She groaned as she tried to get her legs up under him to kick him away.

"Look, fat-ass," she hissed, "I can't move my legs."

He lifted a gnarled claw and Stephanie's eyes grew wide, figuring that was it. She clenched her eyes shut, waiting for the blow, but it never came. She slowly opened one eye, staring curiously at the demon's face. His mouth was open and his eyes were protruding; he was clearly in pain. She looked at his chest, where the end of a blade was sticking out. Above them was Calvin, who gripped the sword with both hands and pulled it back out. The demon squealed and turned to dust, blanketing Stephanie.

Calvin reached down to help her off the floor, grabbing his gun and turning as a demon raced toward them. He aimed carefully and pulled the trigger, catching the demon right between the eyes. He wobbled back and forth for a minute and fell backward, turning to dust before he hit the ground.

"Thanks," Stephanie told him as she stood up and brushed off the dust, starting with her face.

Eric walked toward the three demons moving around on the stage, who snarled and jumped to the floor holding their guns at their sides. As the Killers approached, the demons froze and looked at the elevator.

The elevator dinged and a deep, growling voice bellowed across the theatre, "*Esaeu lizz ozz gia. Burning ir ya depths aem sazz maen* eternity."

Stephanie looked at the demons, who threw their weapons to the floor and put their paws in the air. They began to slowly morph back into their human forms, trembling in fear.

The doors opened and Katie walked out with a big-assed smirk on her face.

"Hey there, guys. See you've got your hands full."

The demons growled and reached for their weapons when they saw that they'd been fooled but Eric kicked a gun across the floor, pointing his own at the demon it belonged to. Stephanie and Calvin stomped hard on the other weapons, crushing the demons' fingers beneath their boots. Stephanie looked into the burning red eyes of the beast in front of her and smiled.

"Please, try just a *little* harder and my finger will—whoops—slip, splattering your brains all over the floor." Her eyes flashed. "I'm not a cop, so you'd be making my day."

9

Moloch looked out at his office window at the droves of demons lined up outside. They growled and snarled, some of them with battle axes, others with swords, and the rest with nothing but their razor-sharp claws.

They were ready for battle, and Moloch wondered what T'Chezz had told them or bribed them with. It didn't matter to him, though. *He* wasn't the one who would have to stand behind whatever promises had been made when the war was over.

He returned to his desk and lowered his large body into the chair and looked up at T'Chezz, who stood with pride in his bright red eyes.

Moloch's eyes shifted to the sharp claws drumming on his desk, the marks in the wood from his talons getting deeper with each contact.

"How many are there?" Moloch asked, keeping his voice neutral.

"A thousand, give or take." T'Chezz walked to the window and looked at the sea of demons. "They are ready to take down these humans and to take over the cities aboveground—once you open the gate from hell to Earth, of course."

"Good, but my men go in first. I want them to lock down the initial town to make a safe entry point for your army. Once it is clear you can release them. I am assuming they are not as well-kept as those in human bodies?"

T'Chezz shrugged. "Not so much, but they can take instruction and are bloodthirsty and ready."

"Then it's vital my men go in first. They can help guide the demons."

T'Chezz rubbed his chin, still staring at the army in front of him. He could feel the thrill of war in his fingertips and the taste of victory just on the edge of his reach. He was done playing games. Things needed to escalate so the humans and mercenaries would know that hell was coming to Earth and there was nowhere to hide.

T'Chezz walked over to Moloch's desk and dropped his voice. "I want the world to know that there is going to be a War of the Damned...and they have been invited to die!"

Moloch nodded slowly. "And that is *exactly* what we will do. You just have to keep your patience intact. It won't be long now. The groundwork is being done, and the demons will have their day on Earth."

T'Chezz smiled as he sat down in the visitor chair and ran his finger along the edge of the desk. Lilith went through his mind and he smirked, knowing she would eventually be there for him to kill.

She had receded to the back of his mind until that

moment, but he now was ready to exact some revenge and throw her into the depths of hell—if Lucifer himself didn't want her. He looked up at Moloch, who continued to strum his claws as he stared into space.

"I was sad to learn that your plan for the games was uncovered so soon. Your men had started to wreak havoc on those mercenaries, though I heard *she* made an appearance."

Moloch rolled his eyes. "Yes, well, that will all be accounted for in the very near future. Now, if that is all, I have some lunch plans. I will let you know when we are ready to go. Until then, make sure your army is up to speed and ready to go. There could be nothing worse than the useless slaughter of so many Damned at once."

T'Chezz's smile melted from his face as he looked at the army, then he nodded and walked from the office.

Moloch let out a deep breath and leaned back with clenched fists. T'Chezz drove him nuts. Everything he did was done with malice, even toward Moloch. He was getting too big for his britches, but Moloch figured it was only a matter of time until he would take care of *that* little issue as well.

Moloch's doors opened and Baal walked in, tossing a puppy into the air. His eyes following the squiggling little ankle biter until it came back down and his jaws grabbed it out of the air with a quick 'yip,' swallowing it whole.

He looked at Moloch and held out a basket of little furry dogs, lifting his black eyebrows.

"Want one?"

Moloch waved him off and resumed looking out the window. Baal stood crunching away as T'Chezz commanded his troops to march off. Moloch rubbed his face with his hands and turned back to Baal as he blew fur from his mouth, which floated down onto the desk. Moloch rolled his eyes again and shook his head.

"Between T'Chezz and you, I feel like I'm surrounded by complete morons."

"Hey," Baal told him through a mouthful. "You are the one who invited me here for lunch. Don't take out your hatred for that pain-in-the-ass on *me*."

"He is getting too bold, Baal. Too bold." The beast walked behind the troops, disappearing into the lava pits and Moloch's eyes burned red.

Baal watched in amusement as he finished his lunch.

He couldn't *wait* until T'Chezz got what he deserved.

Korbin stood in the entry to Joshua's building watching everyone work their asses off. It was hotter than hell in there, and Korbin made a note to get some kind of cooling system that could handle the heat the large number of machines were putting off in the enclosed space. Joshua waved at him from across the room and he returned his wave.

He wasn't there to interrupt, he just wanted to see how everything was going. Stephanie had been reporting to the numbers him almost daily, but she never mentioned the workers and their quality of life.

He left the building and squinted through the blowing sand. There were military helicopters somewhere close by.

The beat of the rotors echoed across the dunes and

Korbin turned until he spotted two Black Hawks racing toward the base. He put his hand up to shield his eyes from the sun as the main chopper positioned itself over the landing pad and hovered for a moment before dropping onto the pad. The other chopper stayed in the air and circled the base.

That could only mean one thing. The general had come for an unscheduled visit.

The door to the chopper flew open and the general was escorted out by two armed guards. Korbin jogged over to greet him and steered them inside a maintenance building right next to the landing pad.

The general took off his cover, brushing the sand from it as he chuckled. "I tell ya, it's like being back in the Pit."

Korbin frowned. "General Brushwood, this is a *surprise*. What are you doing here today?"

He put his cap back on. "I came to speak to Katie if she is available."

"Oh, sure, sure. She is actually up on the cliffs across the property. She finds it is easier to train out there where it's quiet, and she uses a special staff that requires a lot of concentration. I can send one of my guys out there to get her for you."

The general shook his head. "No need, just have someone drive me out there. I won't take too long with her. I just have a couple of questions for her. Colonel Jehovivich is still in the chopper. Maybe you can show her around the new facility with the rounds to keep her busy. Keep her attention *here* while I am out there."

Korbin shrugged. " Sure, I can do that. Come on, we'll get you a vehicle."

When they walked out of the building, Joshua was standing there looking confused. Korbin put his arm around Joshua's shoulder.

Joshua looked at Korbin, his eyes open a touch wider than normal.

"Can you drive General Brushwood out to the mountainous area to where Katie practices?"

He looked around. "Sure? I thought they were here to pick up a load. I was puzzled."

"No, no." The general patted Joshua on the shoulder. "We got your delivery yesterday. Primo stuff. Good job."

"Thank you, General. Come this way and we'll grab one of the vehicles."

Korbin nodded and Joshua walked off with the general. He wondered what the man needed to talk to Katie about, hoping it had nothing to do with Pandora's appearance at the hotel fight. It would *definitely* be interesting to try to explain to the general, especially since he still wasn't completely in the know on how the whole Damned mercenary thing worked. He didn't understand the humans' relationships with the demons inside them, or that they were on the good side.

Korbin shrugged and headed back to the chopper to meet with the colonel. He hated surprise drop-ins and he didn't have a clue what was going on in the facility, but he would do his best.

He held out a hand for the colonel to shake. "Colonel. The general asked me to show you around the arsenal—the weapons facility—while he took care of some business."

Jehovivich couldn't keep her surprise hidden. "Oh. Okay, I guess I'll do that, then."

As they walked toward the building the sounds of the machinery operating grew louder. Joshua took off with the general in one of the base's off-road vehicles, with the general's two soldiers in the back. Jehovivich looked concerned but smiled at Korbin when she turned back to him.

"Any idea what all this is about?" Korbin asked her as they walked to the manufacturing building.

"No, none," she admitted.

Korbin held the door to Joshua's building for the colonel as she entered.

Stephanie walked around the corner and stopped when she saw the two of them walk in. She cleared her throat and straightened her blouse as she walked toward them. She thought she'd heard choppers, but she wasn't expecting any visitors so she'd dismissed it. Korbin leaned in and whispered into her ear as the colonel scoped out the building.

"Brushwood is visiting Katie for unknown reasons. We gotta keep this one entertained."

Stephanie shot him a concerned look, but Korbin just shrugged and sighed. "Never a dull moment around here."

As Joshua drove toward the mountain that Katie's truck was parked halfway up, the general leaned back to his two guards.

"I want you to stay with Joshua when I go up to talk to Katie. She doesn't much like an audience, and this information is above your pay grade."

The guards exchanged glances, then looked at the general. "We are supposed to stay with you at all times, sir."

The general held up a hand to halt the protest. "I know, but you *will* break protocol just this once. Understand?"

"Yes, sir."

"Good." The general turned back around, wondering if he was right. Wondering if things were even more complicated than he had imagined.

Katie rolled across the gravel and pushed her staff outward with a grunt, then stood up and bowed, brushing the dirt from her pants. She laid her staff on the ground and bent forward, starting her normal end-of-workout routine. She would do ten burpees, as many sit-ups as she could manage —usually around a thousand—and round it out with back-and-forth sprints.

She breathed in through her nose and out of her mouth as she counted down each exercise. On her last sprint back she put her arms in the air over her head and paced back and forth to catch her breath.

This shit is nuts. I can't believe I now work out like this. I thought my volleyball coach was hard on me back in the day.

Shit, from the way you smashed out those burpees it looks like you had a wimpy bitch for a coach.

She walked over to where she'd left her water and took a good long sip, then put the cap back on it and looked out over the valley. A hawk screamed above her.

I wonder what it's like to be a bird?

I don't know. I've never been one.

When you come back to Earth, can you inhabit anything?

Pretty much, although you rarely find a demon who wants to be in anything other than a human. There is not enough power in being an animal, while if you're a human you get to enjoy luxuries you don't find in hell. You may already know this, but demons like food, money, clothing, and all the commercial aspects of human life. All the things your churches call frivolous.

Yeah, well, I like em' too, but not as much as most demons.

I know. Pandora groaned. *It's like pulling teeth to get you to buy a new bra.*

I just think there is more to life than stuff.

Like what?

Katie thought for a moment. *Relationships, kind gestures, and doing for those who can't do for themselves. Then there is seeing places—traveling and visiting all the wonders of the world. You are only here once, I think, so why not see everything you can. Fall in love, be alive.*

I like where you are going with that. The only problem is, you do none of those things.

Well, I was planning *on it before you came around, but things changed. I'm sure one day I will have the chance to do that stuff. I mean, look at Stephanie and Korbin. Neither of them thought they would ever have a chance at love again, and they found it.*

Pandora snorted. *A lotta good* that *does. They fell in love just so one day they can watch each other die at the hand of a demon. I'm telling you, if Stephanie goes first Korbin will finally lose it and go postal on someone.*

Maybe it won't always be that way. Katie shrugged. *I'd like to think that the two of them will have a chance in the future.*

That's what fuels you humans: hope.

Yep, and the hatred of demons. We like revenge; it makes for a good storyline.

Hey, we have that *in common. I* love *revenge. Unfortunately, so do the rest of my kind—like my husband and my shithead brother. Those are the assholes you gotta look out for. They have some deep-seated centuries-old shit going on in their heads. Talk about holding onto a grudge! Those boys are the captains.*

Katie flipped her staff over in her hand with a smile. *That's why we are training—so I don't have to worry about facing them. So that facing T'Chezz will be a walk in the park.*

Pandora snorted. *A walk in Central Park at midnight with pigtails and a shiny purse.*

Katie laughed, then turned when she heard something in the distance. She shielded her eyes from the sun and squinted out into the sand dunes. A plume of dust rose into the air behind one of the off-road vehicles as it sped toward them.

Pandora reached out with her mind.

It's the general. Seems like it's going to be a big-reveal sort of day. He wouldn't be coming here to wish you well and bring cakes and tea, by any chance?

No. Friends or not, Katie gripped her staff tighter in her hands, *we aren't going to be put into R&D, Pandora.*

Huh, you got that *right. Forever free, bitch.*

F our soldiers ran in rank up the steep incline of the trail. They were dressed in full fatigues, their boots laced tight and their packs on their backs. These four men were hard-nosed full-on beasts, and in order to stay that way they trained harder and longer than most in the Army, or anyone else in their group.

Their nine-mile run that day was coming to a close, but they were ready for whatever would happen next.

They had been on hold since their last assignment, patiently awaiting their new orders.

MSG Jeff Morris, head of team operations and Intel NCO, kept the group in cadence as they ran up the steep hill. A larger company was running toward them.

These guys were fresh out of boot, running in their Army-green PT gear. They stared at the four with awed expressions but passed without acknowledging them.

Here ran legends, none of them really belonging to any company except their own. They were sent in on the toughest and darkest assignments, sticking together from chow to battle.

Once the booters had passed, Morris cleared his throat starting their running cadence over from the beginning.

"Above the land,
Across the sea,
We're everywhere,
We need to be.
We're brothers of,
A special kind,
A better band,
You'll never find.
Band of brothers,
That's what we are,
Fighting evil,
Near and far.
Band of brothers,
That's what I said,
Baptized by fire,
Scarred by lead.
We're lean and mean,
And fit to fight,
Anywhere,
Day or night.
When bullets fly,
And rockets fall,
We'll stand our ground,
And give our all.
We're on the move,
We're on the march,
We're diggin' ditches,

And breakin' starch.
When you hear,
Our battle cry,
You better move,
And step aside.
Band of brothers,
That's what we said,
Mess with us,
We'll shoot you dead.
Band of brothers,
Trained to kill,
If we don't getcha,
Our sisters will."

By the end of the cadence all four men had reached the top of the hill and slowed down to fall out of formation.

Morris patted SFC (P) Matthew Brown on the shoulder, giving him a nod.

The guy was more than satisfactory in appearance: always pressed, always neat, always on-point. He was the group's weapons specialist and often knew more about military arsenals than the companies that built them.

Next to him was SFC Eli Davis, the comic of the group. Compared to the rest of the Army he was serious as hell, but with the guys he cracked the jokes that kept the mood light.

He was their engineering specialist, and he could do just about everything they thought of when it came to structures, bridges, and combat support.

Except how to build a bridge out of nothing but sand and a few drops of water from their canteens in Iraq one time. It caused them to walk an extra five hours around the obstacle while everyone bitched at him the whole time for not producing a bridge out of his backpack.

Under their breaths, of course.

Last but not least, wiping the sweat from his forehead was MSG Michael Wilson, the medical specialist. He kept the guys alive, and because of that, he was the most important member of their team.

He was protected at all times, even just out and about on leave. He kept it together with a sense of calm most people didn't have, especially when it came to stitching people back together and pulling bullets out of limbs mid-fight.

They were a lethal team.

The four men eyed a guy jumping out of a jeep and heading up the hill.

Davis spat to the side as his breathing evened out. "Bet you he's coming here to grab Wilson for sticking his pecker in the wrong hole."

Brown sighed. "Told him that tree was a waste of time. Nothing but splinters."

"It was an elm, and it was as smooth as if someone had sanded it with 800-grit sandpaper," Wilson shot back.

The young guy was panting as he climbed.

Davis chuckled. "You might have to deliver a little mouth-to-mouth when he gets here. And I've heard tell that there is a new colonel who has three daughters...last name 'Elm.'"

Three of the men chuckled. Wilson just shrugged.

Finally the time had come. "Master Sergeant Morris," the private barked, standing at attention.

"Yes, PFC, at ease."

He nodded to the men. "Colonel Browder wishes in to see you his office right away, Sergeant Brown, Sergeant Davis, and Master Sergeant Wilson. He has your reassignment."

"Thank you, Private."

Morris turned back to the guys with a smile on his face, knowing what that meant.

It was time for action. Time for them to see more than just the backside of the base. These four men were war heroes who had dedicated their lives to the Army.

The last thing they wanted was idle time on base, just waiting around until the shit hit the fan. But they couldn't have expected what the colonel was about to tell them.

They stood at attention in a row, their covers under their arms as they waited for the colonel to put them at ease. Colonel Browder looked up at the men and stood, then paced back and forth in front of them. He turned and looked Morris in the eyes, waiting for him to flinch, but he didn't. None of them *ever* had.

"You are some of the best soldiers this Army has."

"Thank you, Colonel," Morris replied.

"And for that reason, you are being sent on an assignment unlike *anything* you have ever faced. In fact, none of us has. It has been top secret for a long time, but now we are facing it head-on. You boys will be joining an elite group fighting the worst threat ever to reach our *planet*. Are you *ready*?"

"Yes, sir," Morris and the others barked.

"Good. At ease, boys. Let's have a chat about *demons*…"

The colonel chuckled at the looks of shock on their faces.

Katie poked her head into Korbin's office and gave him a winning smile. He leaned back in his chair and stretched his arms over his head, knowing she was up to something.

She sauntered in with her hands behind her back and looked at him. She had been awfully smug since her conversation with the general.

He ran a hand across his mouth. "All right, spill it. What's this about? I know you want something."

She pointed to herself. "Me, want something? That never happens."

Korbin raised an eyebrow, which caused her to laugh.

"What is it?" he pressed.

"Can you get on the intercom and call everyone to the living area? I think we need to do some soap operas and bonding. It's marathon time, boss."

Korbin rolled his eyes and groaned and Katie gave him a stern look.

"Don't act like you didn't get into the soaps. I forgot to record them and went in to set the timer, only to find you had done it for me. Besides, everyone needs a morale boost."

He leaned forward in his chair. "You know something we don't?"

Pandora urged, *Tell him.*

She nodded. "Pandora says Moloch doesn't get involved unless it's going to go wide. We need to have some fun; enjoy ourselves a bit before the shit hits the fan."

His eyes narrowed, then, "I agree with you."

Katie chuckled, which made Korbin raise an eyebrow. "That wasn't *all* she said, was it?"

"No." Katie laughed. "She said, 'It's time for sugar popcorn, chicken nuggets, and finding out if that bitch in heat got her ten inches from Keven or not."

Korbin smirked as he picked up the phone and pressed the intercom button. He shook his head and cleared his throat before speaking.

"Damian, Stephanie, Eric, Calvin, and Timothy: please report to the lounge for some fun and relaxation, per Katie and Pandora."

Katie leaned forward and whispered, "Tell them to hook up the snacks."

He added, "Katie says to bring the food. That is all."

Katie smiled and stood up, waving for Korbin to follow her. "Come on, bossman. The popcorn is hot and ready."

They walked through the tunnels and into the lounge, where they found everyone waiting for them. Stephanie sat up on her knees and waved Korbin over, snuggling up to him when he plopped down on the couch next to her.

Katie took her normal overstuffed chair to the right of the television, and Calvin was on the couch smirking at the lovebirds. Eric was in the other chair with Timothy sitting on the floor to the left of him, and Damian was in his normal spot in the back.

"You people relax to soap operas?" Timothy raised an eyebrow. "Don't get me wrong, I love me some drama, but I did *not* see this coming."

Eric patted him on the shoulder. "Just go with the flow, man. Go with the flow."

Katie started the first missed episode and relaxed with a

bowl of bright purple sugar popcorn and a plate of chicken nuggets.

She was introducing Pandora to the wonders of honey mustard and had already gone through three packets.

Everyone quieted down as the opening credits faded to a view of Maria, who stared at Keven lying in her bed with a white sheet covering his guy parts.

Timothy snapped his fingers. "Ohhh…that is one hunk of a man!"

Katie giggled as the actors talked about the portals to hell and all the drama they had been through. She looked around the room at the family.

It had changed, but she was happy that she still had one that was *intact*. She'd had to learn that in their world things changed on a regular basis. You either got used to it and went with it—or you fought it, only to find yourself miserable and alone.

She didn't want to be miserable and alone. She wanted all the small pleasures in life she could find, and the six people in that room were exactly that to her.

She looked over her shoulder at Damian, who was intent on the screen as he popped a piece of popcorn into his mouth. He glanced at her and winked.

She turned back to the show and relaxed into her chair, laughing at Eric's and Timothy's side commentary. On the screen, Maria had transitioned from admiring her new lover to arguing with him in a cemetery somewhere. Then a portal to hell opened behind them and out walked Josephine, Keven's wife—the woman he thought had died two years before.

"Oh, hell no," Calvin exclaimed, sitting up and throwing

his arms out. "Push that bitch right back into that damn hole, Keven, and be done with it! She was a real piece of work to begin with. You are free, homie! Free to be with your hot Spanish Mamacita."

Stephanie looked at him with raised eyebrows.

"Not you," Calvin replied with a laugh. "The one on the screen."

Timothy narrowed his eyes. "Mamacita?"

Stephanie shook her head. "Long story. I'll tell you when we do our nails tomorrow. Too long and torturous for right now."

"Mmmhmm." Timothy shook his head and pursed his lips. "Like a regular soap in this place. Who knows what secrets will pop out next? Somebody gonna tell me Big Scary Man over there likes kittens.?"

Katie laughed and looked at Calvin, who just shook his head. Everything was right in the world.

Even if it was just for that one night.

Moloch flexed his muscles as he stepped out of the portal, and looked at Trenton and his team who stood by awaiting his instructions. He walked over to the guys and stared one at a time into their glowing red eyes. Trenton nodded, his hands clutched behind his back.

"Have you been training?"

"Yes, Moloch." Trenton lowered his head. "We are ready for whatever you want to send this way. We have prepared for all scenarios we could think of."

Moloch growled, "Good." He raised his hands to tear

through the air and rip open a new portal, and through the haze was a back alley in a very small town. They all heard children playing in the background. "Go there and sow death, destruction, and *pain*."

An evil smile moved over Trenton's lips as he relayed the command to his team. Their eyes glowed brightly and they began to breathe heavily, their shoulders tense and their teeth clenched. One by one they stepped into the alley, and as the last one crossed the portal slammed shut behind them. Trenton looked at each of them and nodded in approval.

"Behind us was a battle lost, but today begins the *war*. No survivors, unless Moloch tells us to stop."

The mercenary demons took off screaming, grabbing anyone they came in contact with. The shrieks of the innocent rang out through the small Wyoming town as the team killed or maimed all they could find.

Trenton held back, wearing an evil smile as his team taunted the townspeople and laughed as they ripped them limb from limb.

A young boy scrambled out of the library doors and across the street, hiding around the corner in an alley. He pulled out his cell phone and dialed 911, sobbing with fear as he put the phone to his ear.

Suddenly one of the demons came from behind the boy. He grabbed him by the back of his neck and lifted him easily, dragging him out of the alley. Nearby humans screamed and attempted to get to him, but they were put down hard and fast by the team. The kid thrashed, dropping the phone to the ground, and the demon laughed loudly his eyes glowing brighter and brighter.

"No!" the kid screamed.

The Enlightened had *no* compassion. He killed the kid like any other human he encountered and discarded the body.

The boy lay in the slowly-filling pool of blood that washed the street, no longer able to hear the tinny voice of the operator from cellphone beside him.

Trenton walked down the block with his team following him.

The door to the grocery store opened and Brock came running out with his mother in tow.

"Stay there," Brock yelled to his mother as Trenton stood triumphantly on the sidewalk. His hands were covered in blood, and he laughed as one of his team ravaged several older people next to him.

Brock curled his hands into fists and stomped toward him with his anger and his demon's combined. His eyes flashed red as he approached Trenton and shoved him backward. Trenton kept his smile firmly in place, not flinching as Brock threatened him.

"Who the fuck are you? Leave these people alone!"

Trenton broke a piece off the metal bars that formed the cart return and walked toward Brock, gripping it tightly. He could see the red in his eyes, but it was obvious he wasn't on their team.

"You're either with us or you're against us."

Trenton bashed Brock over the head with the metal pipe, blood soaking his hair as he fell to the ground. His mother screamed and rushed to his side with tears streaming down her face.

"You killed him, you bastard!"

Trenton raised his arms to the sky and let out a deep menacing laugh, reveling in the freedom to commit mayhem he had been looking for. These humans were so *weak*. He could barely stand the sight of them.

Brock's pain pierced his nerves, but he couldn't open his eyes. His succubus kept him in place and healed his wounds as fast as she could.

You aren't dying on me, you damned hypocrite! You promised me a date with Super Package back there and I mean to make it happen.

She paused for the tiniest of instants to imagine that package and redoubled her efforts.

There was no way she was going to let some low-level scumbag take *her* human and send her plummeting back to the depths of hell. Whoever these guys were, they had been sent by someone powerful—and the succubus needed Brock alive to figure out who it was.

There was no reason to attack that town, not unless there were bigger plots afoot. She had a sinking feeling this was just the beginning.

MSG Morris, MSG Wilson, SFC Brown, and SFC Davis arrived at a hidden section of Fort Bragg.

As they exited their plane they looked out at the mass of recruits who had been brought in for the special assignment. Nearly a hundred men and women chatted among themselves while they prepared for the general's briefing.

The guys were curious.

This assignment had an air of mystery about it, especially since the details were still being kept secret. None of them really understood what was going on, but they had their speculations.

The four made their way through the crowd toward the back hangar bay where rows of chairs had been set up for the presentation. Armed guards stood watch outside the bay, there to make sure that security stayed tight for the event. Morris' team stood close together, looking at both the oddly-marked ammo boxes and the planes being rerouted to other runways.

"This must be quite the event," Morris whispered.

"It's not like any assignment I've ever been to," Wilson replied as his head twisted left and right, taking in the sight. "I'm sure it will settle down soon. It's good to see that most of our comrades have wartime experience. That was my biggest concern: being stuck with a bunch of booters walking into some hell on Earth scenario."

"Couldn't be much worse than that time in Kabul," Davis argued.

Wilson chuckled. "I don't know, but for some reason I get the feeling this is much bigger than we imagine. I guess we'll find out soon enough."

A group of soldiers to their right gathered in the shade to stay out of the hot sun. They looked at the four men and nodded, then turned back to one another. They were proud to have been chosen for this assignment, even though they had no idea what they would be facing in the coming days.

"I suppose it's about time we started to get chosen for these types of things," one of the master sergeants in the group proclaimed. "I can't speak for you, but I have been working hard my whole military career to be looked upon as exemplary."

"I'm just glad to be out of Fort Jackson. My downtime there was killing me," another in the group responded. "I have gotten so used to action that I didn't know what to do with myself. Do any of you have family?"

All five of the soldiers shook their heads.

"Well, then we're fucked," he commented and the others chuckled.

Being chosen for an assignment that excluded soldiers

with families was never a good thing. By the same token, the ribbons and accolades each of those chosen had received took dedication to the Army and left very little time for things like spouses and children.

They were all fierce soldiers willing to face what came their way.

The guards stepped to the side of the bay doors and began to usher the soldiers in. They filed forward to take their seats in the rows of chairs, nodding at the people around them. When everyone was inside, the NCO approached, clearing his throat.

"Atten-SHUN!"

The soldiers rose and stood at attention, their covers under their arms.

General Brushwood came in through the back and walked down the center aisle to the podium at the front. He nodded and put his hands up, signaling for everyone to take a seat. Those in the seats sat silently, straight-backed in their chairs.

The general cleared his throat and looked around the room at the brave soldiers, men and women, who had been handpicked for the assignment.

"Welcome, men and women of the United States Army. I am General Brushwood, and I will be your leader through one of the hardest, if not *the* hardest, assignments you will be given in your military career. Many of you are wondering what this new assignment is, and to explain further I am turning this over to Colonel Jehovivich."

The colonel nodded at the general and took the podium while packets were being handed down the rows. She opened her notebook and held up a hand as a low murmur of chatter rippled through the bay.

"In your hands are the official briefings which include the history of this new war, as well as details on the enemy —or what we know about them so far—and the allies working with us. You can take your time going through it, but it is important that each of you familiarize yourselves thoroughly with the assignment. I will say this: this enemy is different than anything any of you have faced before. They are literally *not of this world*. The days of joking about a 'hell on Earth' have ended, since this is exactly what you will be facing. All demons are fast and some are extremely intelligent, and they are learning to use weapons we would face in a normal war. Not only that, they are damn hard to kill. I know this is a lot for you to take in—and your commanding officers will be available to answer questions in the mini-briefings that will occur after this one—but please understand that you wouldn't be here today if we didn't think you were capable of killing these sonsabitches and sending them back to hell."

"Hooah!" the soldiers yelled.

The colonel nodded. "I'll turn you back over to the general."

The general stepped back up to the podium, his hands folded in front of him. "Thank you, Colonel." He took a deep breath and looked over the crowd again, The soldiers now looked confused, and a few faces were touched by fear.

"You are not 'the best of the best of the best,'" the general quoted from *Men in Black*. "I wanted the toughest motherfuckers out there. Those who have chips on their shoulders. Those who aren't afraid to go into dark holes and get muddy. Those who can fire a weapon, but protect a child. *DO I HAVE THOSE PEOPLE HERE?*"

"*HOOAH!*" they responded.

Better.

"You are the men and women I label both as killers and as protectors of the innocent, and you have been chosen to face the greatest threat mankind has ever seen. Many of you will not make it out alive, but you will die heroes and we will honor you every day when we march into battle to take out these demon scum and cast them back into hell. I wish you luck and Godspeed, and I will provide anything I can to assist you in your mission. In the coming days you will see the darkness, but we will pull through. We *will* march on, and when we do heaven will shine down on this great planet and on those who risked and gave their lives for the fight. May God be with you."

"Attention!" the NCO yelled.

All the soldiers jumped to attention as the general and the colonel left the podium and headed to the back of the hangar bay. He stopped just inside the door and looked back at the men and women at attention.

"This will be the last time we see all of them alive," he told Jehovivich softly.

Moloch stood in front of the gates and looked at the sea of battle-ready demons. T'Chezz paced beside him, impatient for the next step to begin.

T'Chezz thought *he* had done the work; laid the seeds

and now set in motion the next step toward ending life on Earth as the humans knew it, but Moloch knew better. To him, it was just another step closer to achieving his desires and getting T'Chezz out of his hair.

T'Chezz stepped forward and put his hands in the air to get the demons' attention.

"Soldiers, you stand before me on the edge of greatness. We will be making history in our push toward freedom. Freedom for the demons to claim Earth as our own." He pointed at a spot in front of the group. "When you step through the portal we will create you will look down on a small town, but know that place it is only the beginning of your triumph. Go to that town and take over those people, but do not focus on eating and changing. You need to spread out and make your way across the United States. Take over more cities one by one until we control one of the most powerful nations on the planet. Once that has happened, the world is next!"

The demons growled loudly, the dull roar of their deep voices echoing across the barren lands of hell. Moloch glanced at T'Chezz sideways, thinking the dramatics were a bit much for a bunch of low-level demons who probably didn't understand half of what he was saying.

He let him have his moment, though, hoping it would be the last time he would have to listen to his battle cry to the Republic.

"This is our beachhead, and this is our time!" T'Chezz stepped to the side and nodded at Moloch.

T'Chezz's pleasure at Moloch doing as he wished irritated the higher-level demon. He might be above him in rank, but he knew what was good for him—and taking Earth would be good for everyone involved.

Still, T'Chezz' naïveté gave him some comfort. It prevented him from realizing that Moloch had engineered it all and fooled T'Chezz into believing it was all his doing. Moloch's mercenaries had already cleared the way for the demons, making it virtually impossible for them to screw up.

They were clearly dimwitted. There was no way a goon like T'Chezz could lead them into even a small town and expect it not to be pure chaos, even if the mercenaries *had* taken over the town.

The humans were smarter and stronger than that.

He knew the humans with their Damned and their poison weapons wouldn't be far behind. That was why it was imperative to get the numbers on the ground, even if all thousand of them were sent straight back to hell. It would allow Moloch to clear out some of the human fighters without risking his neck or the necks of his team.

T'Chezz smiled maliciously as the demons flooded through the open portal toward the town now controlled by the demon mercs. He rubbed his hands together as the power surged through him.

It wouldn't be long until he found his place in the Eight in the conveniently open seat left by Lilith.

Timothy's fists balled up. He ground his teeth and stared at the computer screen in front of him that showed the massive flash of energy above the already decimated small town. When Timothy had figured out the incursion he had called Korbin right away.

But he hadn't been expecting to intercept a 911 call from a child.

The child had had no chance against a demon. Timothy's skin crawled as the echoes of the boy's death and the demon's laugh replayed in his mind.

Korbin had called the whole crew in, wanting them to see the damage and carnage so they understood that this would be the biggest call they had taken so far. He now entered the computer room and nodded at Timothy as the others filed in, some sweaty from training, others in street clothing, having been called away from whatever they were doing.

Korbin looked at Stephanie and then around the room at the others.

"My gut told me there was something big approaching, and it was right. The demon mercs have taken over a small town and they are killing everyone—man, woman, and child. Timothy caught the incursion as soon as it began, picking up the spark of a portal in one of the town's blind alleys."

"You'll want to hear this." Timothy sighed and put the 911 call onto the speakers.

"911, what is your emergency?"

"Help us! I'm next to the old grocery store. There are things…beasts every…"

"Hello?"

The screams of a terrified child were followed by a laugh and then silence. Stephanie put her hand over her mouth and shook her head and Katie wrinkled her face in anger.

She looked at Timothy. "How long ago was that call?"

"Not long. Maybe twenty minutes at the most."

Korbin nodded. "We need to get ready and get out there."

Timothy stood up from his chair. "I want to go. I may be a scared punk, but no fucking demon kills a little kid and gets away with it."

Korbin nodded and looked at Calvin, Damian, and the others. He shook his head and whispered to himself.

"War...it's finally upon us."

The whole team left the ops room and through the tunnels to the training room and armory.

They pulled out their bags and began stuffing in ammo and weapons. Katie locked the halves of her staff and slotted it into her back harness, grabbing two pistols and holstering them at her sides.

She also took two special metal knives from the case and slid them into the front of her vest.

"Pulling out all the stops." Calvin's face was set in dark lines. He grabbed a short sword. "These motherfuckers finally went too far."

Katie put her hand on Calvin's shoulder and looked him in the eyes. "Be careful out there. This is going to be dirty, and I need you to come back in one piece."

"You too, and Pandora. She's part of the family now."

Katie smiled and finished choosing her weapons, then followed the others out to the chopper. Joshua climbed in after Katie and buckled his belt, swallowing hard. Katie gave him a tight-lipped grin.

"You okay?"

"Yep. I've shared the secrets with everyone. If I don't come back?" He shrugged. "Nothing will be lost."

Katie nodded and set her bag between her feet. "If you die, I'll figure out a way to get you back so I can kill you myself." The chopper door flew open again and Timothy climbed inside.

He glanced around as he took a seat. "Not sitting this one out."

Katie shook her head. "You boys are crazy, but I'm damn glad to have you."

The NSA headquarters had gradually gotten busier and busier as the numbers of demon incursions rose. They were monitoring all communications and their orders were to find the demon cells and send the info to both military and civilian mercenaries.

It didn't matter to them who cleaned it up, as long as *someone* did.

One of the analysts, a young woman who'd only been on the job for a month, was monitoring 911 calls in areas where incursions were suspected. She clicked on a call and listened and her face went white. She put her hand straight up in the air to attract her supervisor's attention, then took off her headset and handed it to him.

"You might want to take a listen. It's from the latest energy surge, or rather the town near it."

Her supervisor Charles listened in horror as the little boy called 911, only to be snatched up and murdered by one of the demons. Charles gave the headset back and turned away before the analyst saw the tears in his eyes.

Shit like that had never bothered him, but this was beyond too far. The demons were indiscriminately killing everyone in their path.

For the first time, Charles wanted to pick up a weapon and charge into the death zone.

The fucker who had killed the little boy had made a disastrous mistake.

You can kill American men and women and they might seem ambivalent about fighting back.

But you kill a child?

You will get an American-sized boot up your ass no matter what race, color, or creed you are.

The general paused the helmet-cam footage taken at one of the incursions and faced the troops. The screen was frozen on one of the demons. His eyes glowed and his mouth was stretched in a snarl, revealing sharp teeth dripping saliva. The general circled the demon's eyes with his laser pointer.

"You'll see here that the eyes glow red. At this point typically there isn't much left of whatever human the demon took over. Some demons will look like this and others will look like you or me, only with a red ring in their eyes and a shitty attitude."

The general started the video again and everyone watched in horror as the demon leapt high into the air, landed on its feet, and swiped its scimitar claws at a soldier nearby. The viewers were on the edge of their seats when the injured soldier jumped back, raised his gun, and unloaded several rounds into the beast's chest before collapsing. The demon clutched at his chest with his right hand but continued to advance on the soldier.

The general stopped the video again and raised a hand to quiet the murmurs of concern coming from the assembled soldiers.

"This soldier survived, sustaining minimal injury, but many others have not been that lucky. The bullets he shot the demon with were created by a special supplier. They are made of a specific metal, one that emits radiation that incapacitates the demons. Standard ammunition has little to no effect on the demons; they shrug it off and heal the damage. But you can see that this one is in pain. The special rounds prevent them from healing, which allows you to make the kill shot."

A soldier stuck his arm in the air. "You're telling us that three rounds to the chest won't kill those suckers?"

"No, it does *not*," the general replied gravely.

He pressed the play button again, and the scene on the monitor zoomed to show another soldier standing protectively over the injured man on the ground. The soldier shot the approaching demon between the eyes, and this time it crumpled. "You need a headshot, and if you can't do that a good old broken neck or severing the head works too. It's just hard to get that close to them."

The demon hit the ground and morphed back into the woman it had hijacked and the general hit pause. "Now, when you kill one of these sonsabitches, they will either leave the corpse of the human they took, or turn to dust. Intel has told us that the demon itself ends up back in hell to either be sent back here or banished to the depths where it won't see the light of day for centuries."

One of the soldiers raised their hand. "So you're saying that we may, in theory, fight the same demon more than once in different battles?"

"In theory, yes. But because the demon behind this is not Lucifer himself, we are hoping to see the number of demons diminish over time. When you read your packages you will know this has been happening for centuries, but it's only recently that we have seen an influx of demons, unlike anything we've seen in the past. Our job is to let them know we can take them, and that they are better off staying right where they are."

The soldiers were beginning to understand that things were much worse than they had ever thought, and facing these beasts would be no easy task.

The general started the video again, showing the battle to its conclusion. The soldiers gripped their pens tightly as they watched their brothers and sisters die in combat.

In the background of the last clip, a woman leapt over a demon and tore its head off.

The murmurs grew into rumbles. "Who is *that?*"

"Her eyes are glowing!"

"She's killing the demons. Is she on our side?"

The general let a small smile slip at the admiration he heard in their whisperings. "The woman you see is Damned. She is a member of a civilian mercenary group that, after decades of miscommunication, we are now working closely with to win this war. They have demons in them, but they are able to harness that power and use it to fight back. They are the greatest hope we have to win this. They are experienced professionals, and working with them both minimizes our casualties and maximizes the kill count.

"You will even find that on occasion you are running back up for a team of no more than four mercenaries. Those four will take down every demon they find. This particular mercenary is named Katie, and she is the reason you now have the special bullets to use. She and her team have cooperated with the Army at every step, and you are hereby ordered never to cause one of *them* harm under threat of dire consequences—not that I see that as a possibility."

The general snickered to himself as he pictured one of the soldiers in a fistfight with a woman like Katie. It would last all of two seconds before they were unconscious on the ground.

The colonel walked up to the general and whispered something into his ear. The soldiers watched as the two conversed, and the general's face became bleak. When they were finished the general sighed and turned to the group.

"I was hoping we would have some training time before something like this occurred, but there is an ongoing incursion, much bigger than a few hostages in a hotel. There is an entire town under attack. People, it's time to get your game faces on. Report immediately to your squad leaders, who will update you on the latest intel. And troops?" Many in the seats leaned forward. "Be careful out there, and give those bastards *hell*. I'll see you on the battlefield."

The troops left the training room and scattered to make preparations to board the C17s being prepped for takeoff.

They were going on their first mission untrained, but

the general knew there was no such thing as fully prepared when facing those creatures.

They were deadly, ever-changing, unbelievably strong, and had powers only one group of people on the planet had—the Damned themselves.

The general stared at the face of the dead woman on the paused screen.

"Get me the merc teams," he ordered, still gazing at the screen.

The colonel asked, "Which ones, sir?"

"All of them!"

Korbin and the rest of the team had been in the air for quite a while before they received the call to arms from the general.

Korbin called into the conference and listened to the details of the incursion, receiving no more information than they already had. Their intel game had gotten that much stronger since they had brought Timothy on board; Korbin could have called the incursion in before the military recognized it.

He would have to have some discussions with the general when the fight was over, try to figure out what exactly they needed to do to hook the intel teams together.

Before Korbin could relay what he had learned to the team he received a call, which he forwarded to his headset.

"This is Korbin."

"It's Brushwood. Sorry it took me so long to get back to

you. Our new recruits are here, and they're getting ready to take off for the incursion."

"Good. We are almost there; maybe thirty minutes from landing."

"Korbin, an update just came across my desk. There has been another portal opened, and they are calling this one 'the gate to hell.' From the information flooding in from multiple sources there are hundreds, perhaps as many as a thousand, demons running toward the town. They are wild, carrying weapons, and bloodthirsty."

Korbin sighed. "They need to be contained in that town or we risk an attack on a larger city."

The general's tone softened a touch. "Agreed. You will be the first ones there, son. You do what you can, make your lives count."

Korbin grunted. "You act like we ain't got a chance, General. We are Korbin's *Killers*, not Korbin's Kinky Kids."

Timothy's head shot up when Korbin said that. He shook his head and grinned at Katie.

"Wish we were..." he whispered, and Katie smirked.

The general laughed. "Just hold them until we can surround them. The Army is wheels-up and on our way."

Korbin nodded and goosed the chopper. "This we'll defend, General."

He clicked the button on the side of his headset, ending the call, then took Stephanie's hand and looked out the front as they sped toward the town.

This was going to be the hardest fight they'd ever faced, and they might not all make it back.

Timothy looked down at his laptop, his eyes growing wide. "Uh, Korbin, this tiny little town is about to get crushed. The whole infrared just lit up, like there's a giant red blob rushing the city."

Korbin nodded. "That's what the general just said. A second portal—a gate to hell—was opened and they are looking at upwards of a thousand demons heading toward that town. We have to contain and eliminate them and get as many civilians as we can out of harm's way. We are going to be the first boots on the ground, so it's on us to hold them back until the Army can form a perimeter. We have no idea what level or size these demons are, but some of them will have weapons and others... Well, their weapons are built in. I need you guys to stay alert, keep your eyes on each other, and kick ass. I need you *all* to come out of this in one piece. Do you understand?"

"Oorah!" Katie yelled, which made Korbin chuckle.

"That's the Marines, Katie!" he called back.

"It's borrowed." She grinned at him, "I'll come up with one for us later!"

The rest of the team gave an Army-style salute.

Katie stared out the window of the chopper as it raced toward the town, thinking about her tactics and how they could possibly hold back that many demons while they waited for backup to arrive. It seemed like these days they were always the first on the scene, which she liked in some way, but when it came to the safety of her family it wasn't what she wanted.

Take a deep breath, woman. You are making me nervous, Pandora snipped.

This is huge! That's a lot of demons.

Yeah, and you have a lot of demons right here in this helicopter. Look, I'm not saying this is going to be easy, but given how well you guys are trained and with me at your back, you have a real shot of blowing these sonsabitches back to hell. You just have to be tactical about it.

How can we be tactical with demon mercs and demons running amok through the town?

You go in strong and show our powers. You do not back down, and you take out every single fucking demon you can in the process. Let me just say, you cannot bring enough weapons to this fight, so I hope your military friends are bringing the big guns. You are gonna need them to contain this mess.

Maybe you should take over.

Don't go losing your nerve on me now, sister. I am your big gun, and you need to hold me back for when it's really needed. Remember what it does to both of us. We can't go expending that kind of energy right off the bat.

Oh, trust me, I'm not losing my nerve. Just trying to figure out the best approach to save as many lives as possible—including ours.

Korbin will protect Stephanie—you know that—and the rest of this crew is solid, even Timothy. I can feel the rage surging through him from here, and you know that will definitely get some adrenaline going. His demon may be an incubus, and a lazy one, but he won't let Timothy go down without a fight and neither will the rest of their demons. You need to keep your head on straight and not worry about the strong, not unless they are your opponent. Use your staff, use your guns, use your damn teeth if you have to. Get creative, because they aren't going to just leisurely come after you one at a time. They are going to try to mob you. That's how the little ones win—numbers.

Hopefully when they see us fighting they will be slightly distracted by fear.

That's exactly what I was thinking, which is why I'm taking down my blocks and letting any demon who gets close know exactly who I am. That will distract them enough for you to get the upper hand.

Thanks, and I'm looking forward to shoving these knives on my staff straight through some demon scum...no offense.

I'm gonna need some serious donut therapy when all this is over with. Like seriously—we need to find that place in LA that sells donuts as big as your head.

I didn't even know that was a thing.

Oh, hell yeah, it is, and if we ever tie the knot, they make wedding cakes too.

That's so romantic. Katie chuckled.

She looked back out the window and in the distance was the small town they were headed toward. Plumes of smoke came from the center, forcing Katie to squint to see the droves of demons pile in. A dull burning rose in her chest, letting her know that the majority of the demons were low-level.

Still, there were nearly a thousand of them, and it didn't look like anyone in the town had figured out how to take them down yet.

Pandora growled, *Low-level, just like I thought. These puny little bastards are gonna piss their fucking panties when they feel my presence. The queen is back, bitches, and no one wants to fuck with the queen!*

At least not in hell, but shit—pick up a history book and you'll see how ridiculous humans can be, Katie countered.

That does not surprise me in the least. Of course, your queens can't kill you with a look.

You can do that?

Not yet, although I was working on it back in hell. Not all my powers transfer up here, but I have more than most you will face.

Lucky me. Katie chuckled. *No, I mean that...I am damn lucky, or I would have been dead eons ago and your donut habit would have been squashed, finito, done for. I doubt you have delicious pastries on every corner in hell.*

No, but it's damn well hot enough to bake some. Now, get your mind right, bitch, because we are about to have some fun.

13

"The plane's already loaded," the soldier said with frustration in his voice.

"Yeah, with a standard load," another responded. "Obviously this isn't just some standard operation."

"We can't change the loadout until we are ordered to do so."

"Fine, then we'll just sit here and waste time. The incursion started an hour ago, and here we are still sitting here on the ground staring at the rear end of a C-17 with a standard loadout which will do absolutely jack-all for us down there."

"You boys need to stop arguing!" Colonel Jehovivich yelled as she walked up behind them. She handed them a couple of packets. "Here is your briefing and your list for your new loadout. You are going to be facing upwards of a thousand demons; maybe more, maybe less. I want *all* the special ammo we have loaded in, along with the new tear gas canisters and grenades. Be careful with this stuff; it's precious. I also want the Stryker—the one with the mounted autocannons and anti-tank weapons—loaded into a separate C-17. It will land a bit behind us and the guys on that plane will drive it over when it's time. Is that clear?"

"Yes, ma'am," the soldiers replied, peering at her.

"Don't just stand there staring at me, *move your asses!*"

The colonel rolled her eyes and turned to see four men standing off to the side, unsure where they were supposed to be helping. She recognized the lead, Master Sergeant Morris, from his file. He was a badass, hell-bent on justice, no problem pulling the trigger. His men were the same—all the best of the best. Wilson was probably the most capable medic in the Army and would have to crawl around if he actually wore all his medals on his dress uniform. The colonel walked over to the four of them, and they stopped talking and stood to attention.

"At ease. I know your faces and names from the files. The four of you were the first chosen for this assignment. Do you have any questions?"

Morris cleared his throat and looked at the others. "No, ma'am. We are just eager to get out there and start kicking demon ass...ma'am."

The colonel smiled. "That's good to hear, because most likely you will be working alongside me."

Morris glanced at the others but didn't say a word. The colonel smirked.

"That's right...a woman on the front lines, getting down in the dirt with you. You have a problem with that, gentleman?"

"No, ma'am," they replied in unison.

"Good. Now go help those guys with the new loadout. There are Strykers to load, ammo to get moved, and weapons to stock. I want us out of here in thirty minutes. Do you understand?"

All four nodded and took off toward the plane. Morris stopped and looked at Wilson, who was watching the colonel walk away.

"She's got some brass ones." Morris laughed and shook his head. "Not at all worried about fighting alongside her."

"Not in the least," Wilson agreed.

The colonel returned to the general's post, where she found him looking over maps of the town. He circled three main areas in marker, then joined them to put a horseshoe around the whole town. Jehovivich approached and looked down at his work.

"They are loading the planes with the new equipment and ammo."

"Excellent." The general stood up and exhaled slowly. "This is a big one, Colonel. Too big for the troops we currently have. I've called in some backup and they will probably get there before we do. These three areas are where I'll focus our initial efforts; we'll create a horseshoe around the town with the armored Humvees and Strykers. Of course, all this is theoretical since we don't know what impact the mercs will have on the situation before we get there. Damn it all, I wish we could move faster! So much red tape."

"Hurry up and wait, sir," Jehovivich remarked with a smirk. "Besides, there is a time and place for go, go, go, like with the mercs, and one for slow and steady. We win the races, sir."

"Sometimes, but in these circumstances so do the mercs. We will work with what we've got. This town may be small compared to others, but there are houses and farms beyond the marked perimeter. We have to focus our efforts on the most populated section, which is the center of town. God be with the rest of them."

"No one expects to come out of this with zero civilian casualties, we just need to minimize them. Hell, there were casualties before we even heard the news. The NSA has picked up dozens of unfinished 911 calls from men, women, and children, all of them are presumed gravely injured or dead. We are going to get those demons, sir, and we are going to make them pay."

"Damn right we are!"

"Ladies and gentlemen, we have arrived," Calvin belted out, looking down. The demons swarmed the streets below, some carrying bodies and others dragging live people across the pavement.

Katie gritted her teeth and stood up, then pulled out her staff and twisted to split it into two. She looked at Timothy, who was staring at her strangely, and a devious smile moved over her face as she opened the door. Calvin reached up and flipped the switch to the music, blaring it from speakers he had installed on the chopper.

Katie took in a deep breath and looked back at the group, her eyes shining bright red.

"I've got some dirty deeds to do!"

Timothy gasped as Katie winked at him and dropped

backward out of the chopper. He looked out his window just in time to see her turn in the air. She clicked the button to open the blades on her poles as she brought her arms out to the sides, and Timothy's eyes grew huge and he gripped the edge of his chair. He was freaking out by this point, just having watched Katie drop out of the chopper two hundred feet off the ground. He had no idea how she made falling look like an art form.

You might look like a Jackson Pollock when you land, his incubus offered.

Timothy gulped. *"I'm* not supposed to do that, am I?"

Korbin chuckled and caught Timothy's eye in the mirror. *"None* of us are supposed to do that! That's a Katie thing. Don't worry, you'll get to step safely off the chopper onto the ground before you start taking down any beasts."

Timothy let out a relieved breath and resumed looking out his window. He spotted a group of demons with something in their hands standing in a row on top of one of the buildings. Timothy pressed his face against the window to get a better look.

"Uh, boss, I think we might have a problem..."

Korbin looked out the side window just as the demons began throwing boulders at the chopper. He swerved, forcing everyone to grab their seats as it rolled away from the demons. They flew into range of another row of demons on another building, who also sent boulders toward them. Korbin danced his hands over the controls and the chopper dodged and moved through the flying stones, Korbin doing his best to keep the team in the air until he could find a vacant open area to land.

"Mother*fuckers.*"

A huge piece of one of the buildings came flying at the chopper and Korbin dove, whipping back up at the last second. The piece of stone hit the building across the street, sending stones down onto the civilians below.

"Missed me, fucker."

Just then a boulder hit chopper's tail and it spun while Korbin tried his best to keep it under control.

Timothy closed his eyes and gripped his seat. "I'm too young to die, bitches, I'm too *young*! I haven't even seen Cher in concert yet."

Korbin sighed with relief when he spotted a patch of grass in a park just over the hill. He gripped the cyclic tighter, growling as he fought to force the chopper out of its downward spiral. The stick bucked in his hands and the chopper listed back and forth as he pushed it to its limits to reach that spot where he could at least land without taking any buildings out.

"All right, kiddies, buckle in tight. This is gonna be one *hell* of a landing."

Another boulder clipped the back end of the chopper and it tilted forward. Everyone tensed as the chopper sped toward the ground at an angle, not slowing down.

Timothy clenched his eyes shut. "I wish I was religious right now."

The chopper landed at an angle and the blades skimmed the grass, but Korbin was able to pull it back enough to not send debris flying. The tips of the skids scraped the ground as Korbin shut down the engines and the blades continued to whirl quickly, throwing up mounds of dirt as the chopper slid forward.

Time slowed for Calvin as the chopper skidded

toward a sturdy sycamore and his eyes grew wider and wider as they got closer and closer. Finally they stopped and the back end of the chopper slammed down on the ground. The nose of the craft was just inches from the trunk.

Everyone sat still for a moment to regain their bearings. The demons had already put a hurting on them, and Korbin was madder than hell that his beloved chopper was now a twisted ball of useless junk. He slammed his hands on the dash and looked back at the others.

"Everyone all right?"

"Yeah," Calvin replied.

"Does shitting your pants count as all right?" Timothy asked.

Stephanie nodded at him, dabbing at a small cut on her forehead she'd gotten during the landing. Korbin undid his belt and grabbed his weapon. "All right, guys, let's get out of this thing before they swarm us. Remember, keep your eyes open and look out for each other, and if you find that motherfucker with the baseball arm, send him to me. We need to talk about my chopper."

Katie bent her knees as she hit the ground in a billow of dust. She looked up as the chopper blew by with Timothy's silhouette visible through the window. She smiled as she stood up and looked around.

Her heart sank as the dirt settled. There were bodies everywhere, some freshly killed, others half-eaten. Those sonsabitches had opened up hell in this little town, which was obviously their point. She stepped forward but stopped when she heard a sound to her right.

Two demons were growling and snarling as they walked toward her. *Poor dumb bastards think I'm easy prey.*

Pandora growled, *Kick their asses into the ground, and let me have a few punches.*

Katie smiled, leaning her poles down against a bench on the edge of the sidewalk. She dusted off her hands as walked over to them, then pulled her arm back and punched one of the demons right in the face before either of them could react. He flew back, landing in the town's fountain fifteen feet behind him.

Katie turned to the other demon and Pandora juiced her.

"So, you think you can come to my world and to *my* country and do this to *my* fellow Americans?" The demon tilted his head, sensing something strong. "How wrong you are."

Katie grabbed the demon by the shoulders and thrust her knee into his stomach. The other demon came running toward her, having extricated himself from the fountain, but she backhanded him across the face, which sent him to his knees. She turned back to the demon she had just kneed and punched him in the face, her rage growing by the second. The demons wavered, stunned by the force of Katie and Pandora's blows. She grabbed her poles, tapping the blades against her legs.

"Fuckers!" she yelled. She crossed the poles over her body and slashed them down across the demons' throats, and they grabbed their necks. Black blood oozed through their clutching fingers and their red eyes flickered for just a moment, then both of them turned to dust.

Katie smiled for just a moment, then there was a loud crunch. When she looked up the helicopter was spinning; it had been hit by a boulder. She watched helplessly as the bird spun and then wobbled from side to side. Korbin had clearly regained some sort of control, but he needed to get down safely. She pulled a pistol from its holster and shot to the left, killing a nearby demon as it grazed on a body.

The chopper hit the ground and skidded forward before finally coming to a stop in front of a large tree. Katie let out a deep breath and shook her head as she turned back to the street. "Korbin is gonna be pissed as hell."

Katie stepped over the debris in the street, her poles raised for a fight, and when she turned a corner she came across a group of Enlightened backing a couple of teenagers into a corner.

Katie gritted her teeth and gripped her poles tightly.

Fucking demon mercs! I knew they had to be at the bottom of this.

These are the weak ones. You can take them.

Damn right.

Katie banged her pole against a piece of metal on the ground to attract the demon mercs' attention and they turned as one, their eyes bright red and their demon teeth showing inside their human mouths. They snarled at Katie, who just smiled coldly at them. The two teenagers saw their opportunity and took off, but the mercs didn't care. They knew that face. She was the one who killed their brothers in the woods outside the hotel.

"My friends are here too in case you were wondering—and we have had *enough* of this shit."

"You're too late," one of the demons snarled. "Hell has been unleashed. The demons will make it through, and when they do you will watch your entire country burn in hellfire."

Katie lifted her eyebrows. "Well, *that* doesn't sound like something I would enjoy now, does it?"

The merc hissed and lunged at her. Katie swung her pole, barely missing as he rolled to the side. He landed in a squat and leered at Katie. He had her in height and reach, and he was about three of her in width.

Katie was unfazed. "You're a big guy, aren't you? What, like three-fifty? You know what I've learned about the big guys?"

"What's that?"

"The bigger they are, the harder they fall." Katie swiped the blunt end of her staff down and over and knocked the merc off his feet, then jumped on top of him and leaned in, her face just inches from his. "You see, we are *way* tougher than you and your little demon."

Pandora's arm reached out of Katie's chest and grabbed the demon inside the guy, holding it up in the air as it screamed and writhed. It finally disappeared back into the depths of hell and Katie looked at the dead mercenary beneath her. She had never seen an exorcised human fail to recover.

His soul wanted and welcomed that demon. They were inter-twined. None of the mercs are redeemable, Pandora told her.

Katie stood up and narrowed her eyes at the others. *Well then, we'll just have to kill them all.*

14

The local authorities were the first ones on the scene, but from the looks of scattered and torn uniforms in the streets, none of them had stood a chance. They had been lost before Korbin and the team had even gotten there.

They were small-town boys used to petty thefts and the occasional domestic abuse call, so the demons took them down before they could pull their weapons. Two groups of National Guard had been deployed shortly thereafter, but with no training, no special weapons, and no idea what the hell was going on, barely any of them had made it out alive. The few who did made their way to the edges of the town to await backup, tending their injuries in the meantime. It was pure hell in that town; already too many lives had been lost.

The state troopers came barreling toward the town, but before they arrived they were told to stand down and wait for the big guns at the edge of town. They had gone all wide-eyed at the girl jumping from the helo two hundred feet from the ground and seen Korbin's chopper crash land.

"Boys, I can't explain this," the captain told them.

"Maybe they can," one of the officers suggested, pointing at the C-17s landing in the distance.

The National Guard soldier stood up and squinted his eyes. "There's our boys. Army boys."

The captain peered at the insignia on the side of the plane. "What battalion is that?"

"I don't know, but from the looks of the beast painted on the side of the plane, they know a hell of a lot more about what is going on in this town than we do. I don't know about you, but I'd welcome a briefing right about now. I lost all but six of my men down there, and your local cops were just meat for those beasts."

Several choppers roared into the fields beyond the town, hovering for a moment as they surveyed the wreckage of the chopper. Korbin and his team were running, guns blazing from the downed helo. The new arrivals set down on the perimeter and the general climbed out with Colonel Jehovivich in tow.

He walked up to the captain and shook his hand. "General Brushwood. I have to ask that you and your team hold here and keep a perimeter if possible."

The captain looked at the three hundred or so men marching toward them from the planes. They were carrying ammo and supplies. They didn't look like normal soldiers, although they were dressed in regulation fatigues. "What team is this?"

"We are the Demon-RRF, Ready Reaction Force. We

were able to get here quickly, and the army is behind us. We are three hundred strong, including a hundred new members freshly trained and ready for this sort of situation."

"And what sort of situation *is* this, General?"

"Demons," the general responded, patting him on the shoulder and looking at the town below. "Straight from hell. Genuine Lucifer's-stamp-of-approval fallen-from-grace demons."

"I'm sorry, *what?*"

"Long story, Captain, but we'll get you up to speed soon. Just have your men fall in. The colonel here will get them some better ammo to take down these bastards. Anyone with red eyes who's not part of our team rushes you, take them down, bullet to the head."

"How will we know who's on your team?"

"Trust me." The general smirked. "You'll know."

The general turned to Jehovivich. "I want you to brief the few National Guard who are left and get these state police some decent rounds for their guns, then get the RRF spread out. Let's start with the horseshoe formation to make sure none of these bastards get out of town, then we'll assess what comes next. The rest of the mercs should be arriving soon, and I need their eyes and ears on the ground before the rest of the Army shows up. This needs to be smooth and calculated. Ignore the chaos and get this under control."

"Yes, sir." Jehovivich nodded and glanced at the town. Demons were clearly visible, most of them no longer looking anything like human. There were bodies piled in the streets, and screams echoed through the valley.

This was the worst thing she had ever seen during her time in the Army, and she knew it would only get worse before it got better.

Charlotte pulled her car up to the edge of the gravel road and grabbed her camera and notebook. There were soldiers moving ammo and supplies to the front of the wall of men they were building around the town. She had caught wind from one of her hacker friends that there was another demon sighting, but what she was about to walk into was way more than that. She got out of the car and hung her camera around her neck, scanning for Korbin's Killers.

The place was so chaotic that no one checked her credentials; she just walked straight into the center of it. To her right was the general, who was speaking to the state police captain. There was no sign of the local police, and that made her stomach drop. She had seen these demons in action, and for that many first responders to have shown up it must be one hell of an incursion. She shook her head and scooted past a couple of armed guards to scan the town.

Charlotte's eyes grew wide at the sight of hundreds of demons running amok in the town. They were so enthralled and focused on tearing bodies apart that they hadn't even noticed the growing number of military working their way around the town. It was complete carnage and chaos down there. She pulled a pair of binoculars out of her bag to get a closer look and focused on a tall black man on the street.

"Calvin," she whispered.

If he was there, the rest of them were too. She raised her camera and started taking pictures, trying to get the story documented as fast as possible, then picked up her phone and dialed her editor, but hung up when she saw two highly-decorated soldiers pull another one over to the side. She put her camera down and turned her back to them, trying to act nonchalant as she backed closer to eavesdrop on what they were saying.

"It's a fucking mess down there," one soldier declared. "I'm not sure what the general wants us to do, since I doubt there are any civilians left down there to save."

"What we need to do—I heard one of the colonels talking about it—is clear the whole town. That will keep the situation under wraps and we can focus on saving the people who might have a damn chance elsewhere."

Charlotte swallowed hard and walked away, unsure what they had really meant by clearing out the whole town. There were a lot of different possibilities, but the one that stuck in her head was blowing everything and everyone up. Clearing the way for progress in a hopeless situation. That wasn't something she could fathom—killing innocent people, not to mention the mercs who were down there fighting—instead of going down and fighting with them.

She sighed and stared around, wondering if there was anything she could do to stop them if that was the case. They couldn't be giving up already, not with the mercs down there and more to come, as Charlotte was sure they would. Blowing up an entire town—wiping it from the map—had to be the last-ditch solution; she had to believe that.

If they blew up their own people the demons might lose some, but the bad guys would ultimately win in the scenario. If the hell creatures could force humans to kill their own people, they won. She didn't know how they couldn't understand that.

"I can stop this really easily," Charlotte told herself. She pulled out her phone and called a friend at a news station.

"I have a story for you, and can upload photos and give you commentary on air. I'm sending you a picture right now so you can see."

"Holy shit," her friend responded. "Send over the pictures and hold on—we are going to get this on the air and fast. Good work, Charlotte. Good work."

Charlotte smiled, though she knew the only reason she was calling it in was to save the town from being bombed. She waited off to the side, keeping her movements low-key, and spoke on the air.

"Charlotte, can you describe what you are seeing?"

"A whole lot of military uniforms, Elise. And a whole lot of scary-looking creatures tearing up that little town down there. I couldn't send most of the pictures I took because there's too much carnage. There are specialist teams down there, who came here to get this under control and attempt to get the survivors out of town. It also looks as if they have started to surround the town with troops in order to keep the...uh...*enemy* from escaping."

"Do we know where these terrorists are coming from?"

Charlotte paused, unsure what to say. Was the world ready for that kind of news?

"*Hell,*" Charlotte replied.

"It sure seems that way. That was Charlotte Hillway, reporting live."

Charlotte took the phone from her ear and stared down into the town. "Hell" didn't even *begin* to describe what was going on down there.

The soldiers who had talked earlier about clearing the town watched some demons snarling and growling as they tore a woman's body to pieces below and one of them looked away, grimacing. He had seen some crazy shit in combat—dead bodies and the aftermath of bombings and the like—but he was *not* prepared mentally for what they had walked into.

"What they need to do right now is deploy a GBU-43/B and singe the last remaining hair off these bastards."

"The MOAB? Are you kidding me? There won't be anything left of *anyone* down there," a fellow soldier replied.

"That's the fucking point. That or drop a nuke. We are far enough away from any surrounding towns that the collateral damage will be minimal, even with the breeze today. There is no place for those creatures here on Earth, and we need to send a clear message to whoever is behind this that we aren't playing games. There will be no peace talks; we will just exterminate their entire race and not lose any sleep over it."

"Yeah, because a MOAB is the answer," another growled. "It is doing *so* well for us in Afghanistan right now. What we need to do is save the innocent and start just plowing through these bitches. Show them who's boss, show their master or whatever the fuck they call him that we won't be pushed around. *That* we can handle ourselves with troops on the ground, without backing down or wiping the slate clean. What happens when something like this ends up in Austin or Chicago, or New York even? You gonna bomb the shit out of major cities?"

"No, of course not."

"Then you have to start here. You have to show them that we aren't pussies. That no matter how many of them they push through their little hellholes, we will stand our ground here and anywhere else on this planet."

"I don't know, I think a MOAB would send that message loud and clear."

"Doesn't matter now," one of the soldiers replied, nodding at the mobile command post where the screens were set up. "Looks like this bitch made it to the news already. We can't bomb a town while everyone watches. That window of opportunity closed. We need to focus on the task at hand."

"That's right. We need to get in there and exterminate the demon scum and save anyone we can. I don't know about you, but if their eyes glow my guns are gonna blow."

"Hell yeah, man."

The feeling was the same all across the field as the men locked and loaded their weapons. Their focus was intense, and they were ready for an entirely new level of battle. National Guard brothers and sisters had died, and the ones who were left weren't in good enough physical or mental shape to do any good. These men were damn well not gonna let that happen to the rest of them. They had seen the videos and watched the carnage, and they knew how these bastards operated.

They were ready to start mowing them down.

Trenton stood on the killing ground in town, staring at the bodies with a smile on his face. He looked up the hill, finally realizing that what he called "the spectators" were growing in number and it wouldn't be long before they started pouring into the city.

He and his team had done their job. They had taken the town hostage and opened it up for a major demon incursion. He hoped that, no matter how it turned out in the end, Moloch would be proud of them. They had definitely redeemed themselves after the hotel incident.

The Damned mercs were now racing through the streets and shooting down demons wherever they stood. He clenched his teeth and narrowed his eyes, remembering his fallen teammates. This was the perfect time to exact a little bit of revenge; to make them hurt like him and his team did. Katie and that priest were out there somewhere —he *knew* it. It was time he hunted them down and really showed them who was boss. There were new mercs in town, and they were stronger than before, more motivated than ever, and now they had an army behind them.

It was no longer one squad against the world. This battle was just getting started.

15

The general heard choppers approaching and stepped out of his mobile command post. Half a dozen helicopters cleared the ridge and landed in some fields in the distance. Some of the choppers were military but the others were private, which told him that the other merc teams had finally arrived. He shielded his eyes from the sun with his hand to watch as teams from all over the country jumped out and ran toward town with their weapons strapped to their bodies and their game faces on.

Amy stepped out of the chopper with her relatively green team right behind her. She nodded at the New York teams as they ducked under the rotors and made their way down the hill. Ella stretched her arms over her head, looking around to meet the eyes of the military. She smirked, knowing it was the first time most of them had seen even one of the merc teams, much less the majority of them.

She made her way through the troops, nodding as she

approached the perimeter. She glanced at the droves of demons and patted the gun at her side. Charlotte came up next to Ella and looked toward town, avoiding Ella's gaze.

"Looks like they pulled out all the stops."

"Katie and her crew down there?"

"I saw Calvin, so I am assuming they are."

"Good, and who are all *these* people?"

"From what I can gather from overhearing the general up there," Charlotte nodded toward Brushwood surrounded by the merc team leaders as he briefed them, "it's a special ready response team, all human, no damned, but trained in fighting demons. They will be going in there with you guys, or at least a part of them."

"Ahh." Ella nodded. "Fresh meat. I like it! It's about damn time they stopped sending just any old soldier in there to get his head chomped off."

A soldier standing close glanced at Ella, who gave him the biggest smile she could muster. "No offense. Good seeing you, Charlotte, I'm gonna go get my briefing so I can get down there and start making dust."

Charlotte nodded and Ella walked toward the mobile command post. She looked different, she felt more confident, and the guys were *definitely* keeping their eyes on her. Her tight spandex pants, laced-up boots, and midriff-revealing tank top gave her a sense of badass bitchiness, which was just how she liked it. Her body was muscular and tight, especially after all the health food her demon Melnick had her chowing down on.

She chewed her gum loudly, smacking her lips as she sashayed past the soldiers, then lowered her gold-tinted aviators to show her red eyes and winked. One of the soldiers wolf-whistled and she smiled with the gum squished between her teeth.

"Look me up later! I get horny after I fight!"

Her team approached, laughing at her response to the soldier. They slung their arms around her and led her toward the command post.

"Time to rock and roll. You ready?"

Ella smiled and pulled out her pistol. "I've been ready for a very long time."

Melneck coughed. *Damn right you have, but remember what I taught you. Use your brain. Let our powers surge, but don't go down there getting all showy. I don't want to have to reattach a limb today. That shit would be difficult even for me. Ain't nobody wants a one-armed warrior.*

Shit, haven't you seen Rose McGowan in that movie? Her gun is her fake leg and she kicks ass and takes names. Strap a grenade launcher on me and I'm good to go.

Call me crazy, but I don't think that would actually work.

Ella rolled her eyes. *Always a naysayer.*

Ella's team headed down the hill and rolled into the town hot. They looked at the carnage, shaking their heads, but that shit didn't even faze Ella anymore. She poked at a leg just lying in the street with a bite out of the calf.

These demons are wasteful little bastards.

Eat a whole human and leave the leg? That's not too wasteful. In my day we would devour the brains and—

All right. Ella grimaced. *No need to rehash old war stories. I get the picture. You were a badass human-eating fool, yadda yadda.*

I had manners, and never left carnage in the streets like this.

Well, now you fight on the other side, so get used to it. I'll stick with my greens before biting into one of these things.

Perfectly fine with me. Human is an acquired taste, and I was never too fond of it.

Because you're not really a demon. You're like some weird hybrid.

Either way, shut up and focus! You've got hell to lay down.

Don't have to tell me twice.

One of the Enlightened crept from the shadows and looked around the playground. He still had smears of little boy from earlier on the front of his shirt. He wanted more. He loved to take out the kids; they were the most annoying of all. God's little children were nothing but nuisances to him. They were loud and obnoxious, smelled funny, and always stuck their noses where they didn't belong. The demon was finally in a position to do something about it, so while everyone else was out searching for more people to kill *he* was searching for the kids.

"Come out, come out, wherever you are! I won't hurt you, little ones."

His eyes gleamed red as he carefully stepped through the playground, his boots crunching on the gravel. On the other side of the bushes, Korbin and Stephanie stood guard over the school. The students had been taken to a safe area, but no matter how "safe" people thought it was it wouldn't keep the demons from breaking through. They had to figure out how to get them out and get them to the perimeter without any casualties.

"Maybe they are safest there, and we can lead the demons away," Korbin whispered.

Stephanie put her fingers to her lips and peered through the bushes. On the other side was an Enlightened, and Stephanie *knew* she had heard his voice before. She stared at him for a moment, seeing the blood across his shirt.

"I know that voice," she whispered.

"Maybe on the speaker during the hotel fight?"

Stephanie shook her head, gritting her teeth. "No, that's the motherfucker who killed that boy on the 911 call we listened to before heading over here. Fuck that! He's going down."

Korbin and Stephanie slowly stood and the demon merc growled, drool running down his chin and his skin slightly distorted because the demon inside him was getting stronger. None of the other Enlightened had let their demon take control like that, but *this* demon seemed to have a special taste for the young.

"Oh, look!" the demon growled. "A little older than I had hoped for, but hell, why not?"

Stephanie and Korbin fired at the demon, but he moved faster than any human could, rolling to the side and growling loudly. His hands morphed into claws and his skin turned dark and scaly. Stephanie shook her head and ran forward, jumping high to avoid his claws as he slashed at her. She landed on his back and began to pound his skull with her fists.

The demon bucked, throwing her through the air toward Korbin and the two of them fell to the ground. The demon stood back up and grew taller. His chest heaved with anger as he walked toward them.

Stephanie looked at Korbin and raised her eyebrows. "How about a little teamwork to get the job done?"

"I like the sound of that."

Korbin and Stephanie stood up and ran toward the demon. As they got closer, Korbin slid down on his knees and Stephanie leapt into the air, using his hands as a springboard. She landed on the Enlightened's shoulders once again and Korbin tossed her his short sword. The demon growled and reached back to pick her off while stomping and kicking at Korbin. Stephanie caught the sword and dipped behind the demon's head out of his reach, then thrust the short sword into the demon's head.

She jumped off and rolled across the ground, coming to a stop on the ground next to Korbin as the demon thrashed and screamed in pain. Stephanie took out her pistols and Korbin his rifle. They both aimed at the demon's head and smiled as they fired two rounds each, taking Trenton down to nothing but dust. The short sword clanged on the gravel of the playground and Korbin stood up, then helped Stephanie to her feet.

"Damn good team."

Stephanie nodded. "I would say you are right on target with that one. Best team besides Katie and Pandora."

Korbin smiled and turned toward Stephanie. "I like your hips better."

Stephanie smiled and leaned in to give him a kiss, but before their lips could touch Timothy bounded through the bushes and slammed into Korbin. He was out of breath and pointing behind him. He swallowed and finally got out his words.

"Incoming!"

Three demons ran out of the bushes after Timothy, one with a knife in his side and the others growling ferociously, and Korbin and Stephanie sprayed the demons with bullets. The three demons stopped in their tracks and turned to dust almost instantly. The knife fell to the ground and Timothy walked over, picking it up and flipping it over in his hand.

"Nice. Thought I lost this one."

Korbin and Stephanie looked at him with raised eyebrows. "Oh, did I interrupt?"

Stephanie laughed and put her arm around Timothy's shoulders. "Glad to see you're still alive, buddy. And your hair looks fabulous."

"Thank you." Timothy preened.

"Now let's go kill us some more bitches."

"Yass, girl, let's."

Stephanie and Timothy headed back toward the town. Korbin rolled his eyes and put his short sword back into the harness on his back. He sighed and hurried after them, realizing how much things had changed.

He wouldn't have it any other way.

Brushwood watched from the top of the hill as the mercs entered the town, already putting a hurt on the demons below. For the first time since he had arrived on the scene he let himself feel a small hope that maybe, just *maybe*, they could win this battle. Their main help had gotten there, and he had his hundred to take with him into the town.

The rest of the RRF would hold the line until the Army arrived.

Surely if thirty or so mercs could create that much demon death his hundred could take a huge chunk out of the rest.

He ran back over to the mobile command post, where Jehovivich was giving the last commands to tighten the perimeter. The general pulled off his uniform coat and strapped his holster around his waist. She lifted an eyebrow at him, having seen that Rambo-like look in his eye before.

"General, what are you doing?"

"I can't just stand here and watch. I'm leaving you in charge. When the Army arrives, reinforce the perimeter; close it in as much as possible. No demons get in or out of this town, do you understand me?"

"I'm sorry about this, sir."

"About what?"

The colonel took off her jacket and strapped on her weapons. "You aren't going in without backup, and I've worked beside you long enough to know that you trust me more than the rest of these people."

The general eyed the colonel for a long moment, and finally he nodded. "I am proud of you, Jehovivich. You have some real balls. Now, let's go kill us some demons before the mercs get them all."

The colonel smiled. "Hooah, sir."

They left the mobile command post and ran over to where the new hundred recruits were lined up to await instruction. The general shifted his gun belt and stared at the soldiers.

"We are the elite—"

"Hooah!"

"We are the biggest, baddest Army on the planet."

"Hooah!"

"We are demon killers, and there isn't *anything* we won't do to ensure that every last one of those motherfuckers gets sent back to the depths of hell where they belong!"

"Hooah! Hooah! Hooah!"

"Ready your weapons, ladies and gentlemen. We are *going in.*"

The general marched the troops across the perimeter, calling a halt at the edge of town. The remaining two hundred RRF and the state troopers watched the perimeter for any escaping demons. They stood tall and stayed ready for anything as the general and his troops marched toward the battle. Brushwood smiled, feeling like a Civil War fighting general leading his troops into battle. He raised his gun into the air and fired, and the soldiers yelled war cries and ran past him into the town to take down every demon in their paths.

Jehovivich came up beside the general. "You ready for this, General?"

"I've been ready for this my whole life, and when it's all over I'll retire to some nice sunny island and guzzle drinks made from coconuts."

A demon raced out of the hardware store, stopping when it spotted the general. His eyes glowed brightly and his face writhed as he ran toward them. The colonel raised her pistol, but the general stayed her hand.

"Allow me. I would like to have the first kill."

The colonel nodded and stood back as the general

aimed at the demon. He waited until the beast had almost closed the gap before pulling the trigger and hitting the demon right between the eyes. It turned to dust, which blew into town.

The colonel nodded again. "Nice shot, sir."

"There's more where that came from."

"Then what are we waiting for? Let's show them what the Army is made of."

The general smiled. "Hooah, Colonel.

16

The news reporter shuffled the papers in front of her, unable to fully understand what she was about to report on. When the music came to a stop she stared at the cameraman, who pointed his finger at her.

"We interrupt your regularly scheduled programming to bring you this unbelievable breaking news. I am Jessica Lang, coming to you on this beautiful Tuesday afternoon with some shocking footage. I have to warn you, some of the images you are about to see are extremely graphic."

The screen changed to the images Charlotte had sent: carnage and smoking buildings, blood-smeared streets, and a somewhat foggy view of demons running around the streets.

"These images, as well as eyewitness testimony from a reporter in the field, were sent to our sister station WXBQ just moments ago. There seems to be some sort of battle going on in this small Wyoming town. Here is a live recording from just moments ago."

The reporter put down her pen and waited as the broadcast was played back for viewers. A woman walked up and powdered her forehead. The rest of the studio was stone-silent and no one else moved as the reporters watched the footage.

"We have not confirmed these reports or the reporter who sent them in, but we dispatched a chopper to survey the area. We are going live to Tim Richardson in the chopper. Tim?"

"Jessica," the reporter yelled over the sound of the chopper blades. "The skies have been cloudy around the area, so we haven't been able to get a good look at the town from where we are. Below are two military aircraft, several helicopters, and what looks like soldiers forming some sort of perimeter right outside of town. It's obvious that something big is going on here, although we cannot confirm what it is just yet."

The scene switched back to the newsroom. "Thank you, Tim. We will check back with you as the story develops. We have been able to locate the alleged reporter's Facebook page, where she has steadily been uploading images and reports from ground zero."

The screen scanned through Charlotte's updates, the more gruesome pictures blurred by the station.

"One of the Facebook updates the reporter posted reads, 'So many military, and more on the way. The specialists are on the ground, but no survivors have been found yet.' There is nothing on any of the posts, though, that specifically talk about the perpetrators of the attack. There have been speculations that terrorists are to blame for this attack, and News 7 has our military liaison standing by to comment. Lesley?"

The scene switched to a blonde woman in a business suit standing in front of the White House. She adjusted her earpiece and held her mic in front of her.

"There is currently no comment from the White House or any sources *within* the White House on whether we are facing another terrorist attack on US soil. All representatives have been pulled into a meeting, but the press has been kept out. We really have no idea what is going on, but we will update you as information becomes available. For now, the only thing we know is that the local police in that small town have gone silent. The military has put out a short statement warning civilians in the area to get inside, lock their doors, and stay hidden until the area has been cleared. Cleared of *what*, we don't know."

"It is obvious that something big is going on there," the reporter continued, turning toward the camera in the studio. "From the reports given to our sister station, it looks like some sort of attack by beings not of this world. Is this fake news? We have yet to confirm. The initial reporter is unknown in most journalistic circles.

"We are struggling to understand how this sort of attack could be real. The photos sent in are anything but conclusive, but where we stand those creatures aren't human. We will be staying with you throughout this crisis and bringing you updates as they arrive."

The camera angle switched to the studio and Jessica shifted uncomfortably in her seat. "To recap, there have been unconfirmed sightings of strange beings attacking a small Wyoming town, although the exact location has been withheld to keep the public from wandering into a dangerous situation. The military is on hand, and an unknown reporter has been posting information from the scene. We are going to switch to the weather for just a moment, but we will be back soon with further updates.

Morris, Brown, Davis, and Wilson moved through the open doors of the library. They kept to the walls, their guns raised in front of them. Morris put his fist up to stop the crew and they held there for a moment, listening for any sounds. They heard a soft whimper from inside the main area and Morris nodded to the others. He stayed low as he moved to the doorway and cleared the area, making sure no demons were waiting to jump them.

The others quickly followed, Davis watching the rear. In the center of the room they came across the young librarian, who was hiding under a table trying to stop the blood running from deep gashes in her leg. She covered her mouth and cried as the soldiers moved to her side. Brown, Morris, and Davis turned their backs, keeping watch as Wilson began to tend to her wounds. He had never seen gashes like that before, and he was struggling to get the bleeding to stop.

"What did this?"

"One of those things," the girl whispered through her tears. "They dragged off the people in here and...Mrs. Owens, the head librarian. I don't think they made it."

"Let's get you taken care of." Wilson wrapped her leg after staunching the wounds with fresh gauze. "Then we are going to get you out of here, okay? Can you stand up?"

"Wait," Morris whispered.

The woman sat back down and Wilson grabbed his gun to back up the others. Half a dozen demons scurried through the door and, climbed the shelves, then leered and hissed at the four soldiers, licking their lips. Morris shifted his stance, his M-16 firm in his hands.

"This might get ugly."

Davis nodded. "Fuck these assholes."

He let the bullets fly and the others followed suit, tracking the demons with the sights of their guns. Davis hit one in the back of the skull, and it fell from the bookcase and hit the ground with a thud. Another not too far from Davis jumped out and slashed his arm, knocking his gun from his hand. He looked at the blood on his hand and narrowed his eyes, then grabbed the beast by the shoulders and slammed it to the ground. He seized its head and twisted hard and fast to break its neck.

Morris jumped onto the table and removed the empty clip, taking a fresh one from his waistband. He aimed carefully at one of the demons scurrying up the wall and pulled the trigger, hitting the beast in the back. It fell to the floor, but before Morris could finish it another demon tackled him. They rolled across the floor, the demon's black scales scratching against his hands as they grappled.

He landed on his back with the beast on top of him, snarling and dripping saliva as it snapped at him. He hit the demon in the face, knocking it to the side, then pulled the pistol and jumped on top of the beast, shooting it twice between the eyes. As it turned to dust he whirled toward the demon he'd previously shot, who starting to get back up.

"Like *fuck* you're getting up." He ran over and grabbed the demon by the back of the neck, then pressed the pistol to his temple and pulled the trigger. The demon turned to dust in his hands and he looked back to see how the others were doing.

Brown was standing back-to-back with Wilson as they fought hand-to-hand with the remaining two demons. Blood ran down Wilson's face from a scratch the demon's claw had ripped in his cheek. The demon took him by the throat, his snarling teeth getting closer, but Wilson grabbed his knife from his belt and slammed into the side of the demon's head. The demon screamed and turned to dust and Wilson turned to assist Brown, who was fighting a losing battle. Wilson sidestepped Brown and drew his knife across the demon's throat.

The demon fell back and burst into a cloud of dust. Brown rubbed his throat and shook his head, looking at Wilson. "Thanks, brother. That one had the upper hand."

"That's forty-seven so far between the four of us," Morris recounted. "Let's get the librarian to safety and then *triple* that fuckin' number."

"Hooah, motherfucker," Brown yelled.

Calvin stood next to Eric in the doorway. They had watched the four soldiers taking down the six demons, surprised by their skills.

"Are they Damned?"

"I thought maybe, but no."

"Shit, so they are just total fucking badasses."

"Badasses possessed by the indomitable spirit to fuck up anything that would attack Americans, apparently." Calvin swatted Eric in the chest. "Come on, there's a big group of these bastards across in the park. Let's finish them off and then go find the others."

Eric shook his head and ran after Calvin, glad that there was someone else there who could handle their shit.

Eric and Calvin ran along the side of a building toward the park where they'd spotted three or four demons gnawing on human remains. Calvin looked at them through his rifle scope, grimacing when he saw fingers sticking out of one of their mouths.

"Looks like they are trying to have a nice picnic in the park."

"No time for romance today, fellas," Eric told the demons, taking a step forward, but then stopping.

He pressed his ear against the door of the building to listen to the voices inside. The voices didn't belong to any of their people, and they were talking about killing humans, which kind of clinched it. Eric opened the door just far enough to peek through the crack and saw several demons and a few Enlightened. Eric tapped Calvin's shoulder and moved to the side so he could see.

Calvin peered through the gap for a moment, then swung his rifle around to his back and pulled his knives. "Looks like we just found some of the idiots who started all this. Let's teach them a lesson."

Eric grinned and gestured to the door. "After you."

Calvin kicked the door open, surprising the Enlightened. Eric followed him, raising his gun as a demon dived toward the two of them. He shot it in the head and it burst into dust.

Calvin grinned, twirling his knives. "Looky what we have here."

The Enlightened mercs raced toward Calvin and Eric, attacking as one, and Calvin chuckled as he dodged their hasty punches. He stepped to the side and grabbed one of the Enlightened by the back of his neck as he ran past, growling as he threw the demon merc across the room. The merc crashed through the wall and Calvin followed him, jumping through the hole to land on top of him. He slashed the demon's face and it screamed in agony.

"You come into this town and kill these people?" Calvin growled through gritted teeth. "I'll show *you* what we do to fuckers who pull that shit." He slammed his knife into the demon merc's chest to incapacitate it, then pulled his short sword from its sheath on his back and severed the guy's head from his body.

Eric grunted as the demon merc took him to the floor and knocked his gun from his hand. It skipped across the floor and slid to a stop at one of the demons' feet. The beast looked curiously at it and picked it up, and Calvin watched in disbelief as the demon looked down the barrel and pulled the trigger, blowing a hole right between its eyes. It grunted and turned to dust. Both Eric and the demon merc had paused for a moment to witness the stupidity.

Eric headbutted the merc, breaking his nose. "And you *work* for those idiots?"

Eric got his feet under the merc and pushed hard, flinging him into a pile of stone and rubble, then walked over and grabbed his weapon, dusting the demon dust from the stock. He turned back as the merc groaned and pulled himself to his feet, then puffed out his chest as he advanced toward Eric. With each step the merc took Eric fired, hitting the demon in the chest, the arm, the neck. It just kept coming toward him, grabbing a metal pipe as it approached.

"The head, motherfucker!" Calvin yelled.

"Oh, yeah." Eric chuckled. He unloaded the rest of his clip into the Enlightened's head.

The third demon merc took off up the stairs toward the door to the roof. Calvin sighed and told Eric, "I've got this."

He ran up the stairs two at a time and grabbed the roof door before it had completely closed. He shaded his eyes from the sun as he ran onto the roof. The Enlightened ran toward the edge of the building and leapt to the next roof.

"Where you goin', motherfucker?"

Calvin took off across the rooftops after the fleeing demon, jumping the gaps between the buildings and easily keeping up his prey. Calvin put on an extra burst of speed when the demon reached the edge of the next building and made a move toward the school. He shook his head and pulled his rifle back around.

"Hell, no. Leave those kids alone."

Calvin quickly knelt and propped his elbows on the edge of the building, sighting the demon through the scope. When the demon looked back Calvin exhaled and pulled the trigger, and the bullet flew almost in slow motion and struck the demon merc right between the eyes.

the demon's head jerked back and he flailed his arms as he fell over the side of the building.

Calvin ran to the edge of the roof and looked down just in time to see the demon turn to dust. He returned his rifle to his back and tightened the strap with a jerk.

"*That's* what you get, asshole."

Korbin, Stephanie, Damian, Timothy, and Joshua formed a line as a huge number of demons charged toward them. Korbin lifted an eyebrow and glanced at Stephanie, who gripped her gun and offered Korbin a tight smile. Joshua looked at Damian and then at Timothy, never having seen so many demons at one time.

"At least I know my product works."

"You got like a bazooka or something? That's a *lot* of demons." Timothy had wide eyes and his gun hand was shaking.

"Not so many as all that," Damian told them calmly over his shoulder.

Eighty or more demons formed a circle around the group, and Korbin and the others moved to cover each other's backs and aimed their weapons outward. Damian stood back to back with Korbin, staring worriedly at the snarling teeth around them.

"So...what's the plan?"

"Uh..." Korbin raised both eyebrows and shrugged. "Don't really have one at the moment. Would love input from my team, though. Any suggestions are welcome."

Stephanie pointed her gun and pulled the trigger, taking out three demons in the front row. The ranks closed the moment they turned to dust and the demons scuffled toward them through the remains.

"We could kill three at a time."

Joshua chuckled. "That would technically be fifteen at a time since there are five of us, but I'm thinking they won't just stand around like targets if we open fire."

A demon lunged from the group, his claws aimed at Joshua's head. Timothy turned and fired, splattering Joshua's face with the demon's blood. The demon screamed before turning to dust, Timothy pulled his handkerchief from his pocket and blotted Joshua's face.

"Sorry about that, sweetie."

Joshua wiped his face, then turned toward Timothy and raised his gun. Timothy flinched as Joshua pulled the trigger, catching a demon right in the head, splattering blood on Timothy's face. Joshua smiled and handed back the handkerchief.

"My bad."

"They're movin'," Stephanie called, then looked at Damian and Korbin. "Okay, boys, boost me straight up in the air."

As the demons began to swarm Stephanie hopped onto Damian and Korbin's outstretched hands. With his free hand Korbin shot into the crowd of demons. He hit three or four, which was enough to hold them back for just a second. They tossed Stephanie into the air and she turned a somersault as she flew, spraying fire into the crowd of demons. Stephanie twisted as she came down, both guns firing into the front row of demons, and took down five before landing. Slowly she stood up and cracked her neck, smiling at a gaping Timothy.

The crew battled back and forth, taking down row after row of demons until the beasts got the hint and backed up. Their claws slashed the dirt as they howled and snarled. They weren't giving up, not on this crew; not when they had them surrounded. Korbin pressed back against Damian again, shifting his gun from side to side.

"They've already had a taste of blood. They aren't going to quit until we kill every last one of them."

Damian held his cross in his right hand and pulled out a long sword from under his trench coat. "Then I suppose we will just have to kill every last one of them."

"That's what *I'm* talkin' about." Stephanie laughed as she holstered her guns and drew her sword. The thing was almost as long as she was tall, but for some reason it fit her perfectly. She ran forward, dipping down and sliding along the ground, slicing at the demons' knee level. The legs of four demons were severed and they dropped to their remaining knees. Stephanie stood and her sword flashed in an arc as she brought it down on their necks, removing all four heads before they even figured out what was going on. Their heads rolled around for a moment before turning to dust along with the rest of them.

"That was fucking awesome," Timothy exclaimed. "I gotta train more. Fuck, back off!"

Timothy had turned to look a demon straight in the eye. "Your hot ass-breath is fucking up my chi here. I need you to take two steps back; personal bubble and all." The demon just snarled at him, his teeth dripping saliva and blood. "No? Fine…it's *your* funeral."

The beast growled loudly and a single drop of blood fell from its mouth like a raindrop and splashed onto Timothy's brand-new tennis shoes. His eyes narrowed and he gritted his teeth, then he pulled out a knife and brought it back.

"These are *three hundred-dollar shoes*, you fucking moron!" With that he began to stab, slicing the demon's neck and moving on to the next until he was so out of breath he could barely stand. Stephanie pulled him back into the center.

"Okay there, Machete Man. They are getting pissed."

He looked up as the beasts took another step forward. "Well, fuck. That's a lot of red eyes.

"Dude, seriously—the damn guy was jumping from roof to roof and I was right on his tail. He got to the last one and looked at the school and I was like, *hell no*. So I dropped to my knees, propped up my rifle, looked through the scope and *POP!* Right between the motherfucking eyes. He made a kind of 'whoaaa' noise as he fell…" Calvin made the motions with his arms. "And down he went into a pile of dust."

"Bro, I don't know about that, you seem pretty swole over this whole thing. I mean, seriously…there's no body to prove it."

"Dude, I swear on my grandfather's dick it happened."

"Whoa, whoa! That is *so* against code. You can't swear on another man's dick! Seriously, bro, come on. I have—"

Calvin put his hand in front of Eric and glanced around. "It's a bit too quiet."

The town was a charnel house. There were a few demons to the right of them and some behind them, but there was no longer the chaos they had walked into. The wind carried the stench of death.

"Maybe they all went to the other side of town?"

"No, something isn't right."

Calvin pulled his rifle around in front of him, scanning for any movements in the distance. On top of the hill was a huge swarm of demons, circling something or someone. As Eric and Calvin squinted at the horde Stephanie flew into the air, firing. More gunfire erupted and Calvin's eyes went wide.

"It's the team! They're surrounded."

Calvin and Eric took off toward the swarm, jumping over bodies and sections of buildings that had been destroyed in the battle. They couldn't believe how many demons there were.

"We gotta get in there and help them," Eric yelled over the growls and screams. He pulled his gun and fired it into the crowd of demons.

Eric put his gun away and drew his knives, not wanting to shoot one of the team by mistake, and started slicing throats and breaking necks. He jammed the knife in his left hand into a demon's back and sliced its throat with his right. Calvin yelled to Korbin and the others, but the howling and snarling were too loud; they couldn't hear him. Frustrated he screamed, his muscles tensing and flexing as he picked demons up bodily and threw them to the side to clear a path.

Little by little they made their way toward their crew, some demons turning to dust and others soaring through the air.

Inside the circle, things were getting tense; the demons were closing in. Stephanie wiped the sweat from her forehead and swung her sword again, taking a demon's head off his shoulders. Korbin grabbed another from behind and twisted, snapping his neck. Damian shot several demons, making the sign of the cross with each death. Joshua and Timothy stood close together, shooting every demon who even *attempted* to take a step toward them. Their tactic was apparently working pretty well, since there was a knee-high mound of dust in front of them.

Stephanie looked to her left and a demon flew into the air. She wrinkled her forehead and tapped Korbin on the shoulder, and he brought his knife across a demon's throat and looked up just as a demon bounced off a nearby tree.

"What the fuck?"

The disturbance got closer and a final demon halted in its tracks with its eyes wide as the tip of a sword erupted through its neck. The demon turned to dust, revealing Calvin behind it with the sword in his hand and a grin on his face. He wiped the dust from the blade.

There was a choked cough behind him and Calvin turned. Eric took two steps toward him and held his hand out to Calvin, the other clutching his chest. Calvin followed the line of Eric's body down to his fingertips, where he saw blood.

Blood was dripping from Eric's hand.

"Eric!"

Calvin pulled him into the circle and began looking for the injury. He turned his friend over and found an entry wound in his back. It was from a claw; a damned demon had stabbed him in the back.

Eric coughed blood, and it ran down his chin in bright red bubbles. Calvin caught him in one arm as his legs gave way and used his free hand to fire three successive shots into the head of the demon who'd attacked Eric.

"Eric needs help *now!*"

Katie grinned as she lowered her gun. She made a "come at me" gesture and drew a line in the dust with her foot and the demon growled, blood dripping from its fangs. He threw the human head he had been munching on to the side and lunged for her, and she punched her staff's blade through the demon's face and out of the back of his skull.

Katie grimaced and shook the staff to try to get the demon's blood and brains off. Finally it turned to dust and she lowered her weapon, looking around the house.

"This house is clear," she announced in her best southern accent.

Pandora cut in, *Katie, get outside. The team is in trouble. Someone is hurt, I think.*

What, are you psychic now? Katie ran toward the front door, kicked it open, and ran into the empty street. *Where are all the fucking demons?*

A burning sensation churned through her chest and she turned to a huge number of demons circling prey on the hill. Whoever was in the center of that was in a hell of a lot of trouble. She started to move toward them and was about to pull her guns when she heard Calvin's voice.

"Eric needs help *now!*"

White-hot fury burned through Katie.

She tore up the hill and into the crowd of demons in a killing rage. Pandora reached through her chest, dissolving demons as she passed while Katie snapped necks and kicked ass, taking no names and giving no fucks whatsoever. She whipped out her staff and swung wildly, her progress through the crowd marked by the screams of dying demons.

Pandora dissolved a demon even as Katie's staff smashed its spine. *This is taking too long!*

Well, what do you suggest I do? Fly? Katie paused to sweep the legs from under a demon before stabbing it through the skull with the blade on her staff. *Actually, that gives me an idea...*

She cleared her immediate area with a wide sweep of her staff.

What are you doing?

Katie didn't answer, just bent low and wound up for a jump. She pushed off as hard as she could and sprang over the demons, and even *she* was surprised by how far she traveled. She landed on top of the front row of demons, making sure to stamp extra-hard on the ones who screamed and whined under her feet as she climbed down.

She rushed to Eric's side and bent down next to Calvin to examine the wound, which was oozing blood onto the ground.

Katie looked up at Korbin and his face told her everything.

Stephanie stole a glance at them but continued to fight off the demons, worry on her usually-poised face. Timothy gripped his gun tightly in the center, staring down at Eric with fear stamped on his face. Katie could tell this was his first time in a real battle, and what a first battle it was. She had never seen so many demons in one place at one time. She didn't have time to talk him down, though. Eric needed help, and he needed it fast.

Calvin pressed his shirt hard against the wound and bent to and whisper into Eric's ear, begging him to stay with them. Katie realized that all the loss they had suffered over the months had gotten to Calvin a lot more than she had thought. She could see the desperation in his face; the need to keep Eric alive no matter what. It tore her heart in two, and she could feel even Pandora's pity at the situation. She put her hand on Calvin's shoulder, turning him toward her. "I know you want to help him, but to do so you have to let me take him."

Calvin looked up at her and nodded, his expression showing pure agony. Katie bent down and mustered her and Pandora's combined strength to cradled Eric in her arms, then vaulted, clearing thirty feet of writhing and snarling demons. She looked at Eric, who was choking.

He stared up at her in fear.

"Don't you motherfucking die on me, asshole!"

Several of the demons pursued her as she made her way toward the perimeter, where she knew she could get Eric the help he needed. She glanced over her shoulder and picked up the pace, determined to outrun them. Demons were fast but Pandora was just a bit faster, which kept them off her heels.

As she ran a shot rang out and Katie risked another glance behind her. A demon fell to the ground and turned to dust. Several more fell as more shots rang out and she returned her focus to getting Eric to safety, mentally thanking whoever was helping her.

In the bushes Ella swished her ponytail to the side and kicked away the smoking shells at her feet. She narrowed her eyes to squint at the merc running through town carrying one of Korbin's men. She was fast; faster than any human or demon Ella had ever seen before. It almost looked like she was fluctuating between two different bodies as she powered toward her destination with the man in her arms.

"Is that… Is that *Katie*?" Ella stood up with her rifle in her hand as the woman made it to the line and handed over the merc in her arms. "*Damn*, she's good."

The general breathed heavily as he fired the last round in his magazine and crouched behind the crumbling stone fence. The colonel handed him another magazine and clicked it into place.

"That was number forty. Colonel. We are kicking some *major* ass."

"A lot more to go, sir."

They both stood up and aimed their weapons at the masses of demons running through the lower part of town. They had shifted their focus. Finding no more fresh bodies in the center of town, they had moved on to the lower end where all the family neighborhoods were situated. It was the second place the general had circled on his map. He knew exactly where those bastards would end up, and at that moment it was perfect.

When they had exhausted those rounds they ducked back down to reload, completing the task as fast as they could. The colonel wiped her face on her shirt and looked at the general, who was beginning to tire. He *was* older. He'd been in the trenches numerous times, but nothing as burdensome as this day. The colonel was about to say something, maybe recommend going back for water and more ammo, when there was a scream.

Both the general and the colonel stood up and a shrieking child ran toward them with his mother close behind. The child couldn't have been more than five or six, and the general opened his arms ready to catch the terri-fied little boy.

The two had almost reached them when the colonel put her hand on the general's arm and pushed it down, then raised her gun and fired a shot into the mother's head.

The general lunged forward to scoop the boy up and ducked back behind the fence. He glared at the colonel, whose eyes were fixed on the mother.

"Colonel, what in the hell did you do?"

The general opened his mouth to continue, livid that she had shot a woman as she was running to safety, but something about the staggering woman made him pause—and she teetered back and forth for a moment before turning to dust. His mouth fell open and he looked at Jeho-vivich, who looked at the child. The general nodded and picked the boy up in one arm, using his free hand to fire into the crowd of approaching demons.

The child wailed, scared to death, just having watched his mother die. The general was disgusted that something so terrible could happen right in front of them. A demon had taken away that woman's life and left her orphaned child crying in his arms. He had seen some terrible things in his day, but they had all been conscious choices by the perpetrator and those enemies had paid the price.

This, though…. This was senseless; evil beyond compare.

He emptied his clip and holstered his weapon, shushing the child in his arms. He pulled his other gun and looked at the colonel.

"I shouldn't be doing this, I don't belong out here in the field. My job is to lead, and these men can't move forward without that. This will be the last time I ever see combat, and I am not at all sad about that."

"Understood, and probably the best choice you could make."

The colonel turned to the general and put her hand on his shoulder, glancing at the little boy with his face buried in the general's shoulder.

"I promise, sir, you will make it out of this alive. Right now we need to get that little one back to the perimeter, get him seen to, get some more ammo, and take a moment to regroup. We can't even tell which way is up from here."

The general nodded. "Agreed. And thank you—I know that was a hard shot to take."

"Sometimes we have to make tough choices, and I have come to the understanding that in *this* war there are no easy choices. We need to protect the innocent no matter what. That was what I was thinking when I pulled that trigger: that sweet little boy's face and the faces of all the innocents who have died here today. War is a bitch, but I won't let it take me down."

Charlotte snapped a few more pictures and scrolled through her shots. All the demons were blurry; she was just too damn far away. They had warned her to stay on or behind the perimeter, and though she had bent that a couple of times to get a shot, she didn't want to go too far and end up a casualty of friendly-fire. She groaned and looked at the hill, where a mob of demons circled around something, but she was too far away to see what.

Katie had sprinted to the perimeter and handed off one of her teammates to the medics just moments before. Charlotte had tried to get her to drink some water and rest for a moment, but she had been too worried about her team.

She had taken a few pictures of Katie as she ran off, pictures she couldn't--—and *wouldn't*—ever show the world. Everyone thought Katie was dead. In fact, the world thought *all* the mercs were dead, and Charlotte made a mental note to keep them out of the shots.

She sighed and raised her camera to her face again, pointing it at the center of the town, which was pretty quiet by that point. The general emerged from behind a building carrying something in his arms and the colonel covered them as they made a run for the perimeter. Charlotte squinted again and focused on them, realizing it wasn't some*thing* he was carrying but some*one*.

A little boy was clinging to him for dear life.

Charlotte fumbled in her pocket for her phone and opened her Facebook to start a live stream. She zoomed in to show the general bearing the little boy to safety. He ran fast, bullets flying behind him as the woman with him took out one demon after another. Charlotte kept her camera focused on the general and used her free hand to hold her other camera up to snap random still pictures in the hope that one of them captured the essence of the moment.

One after another people started to join the live feed, and she realized that the general was going to be a hero overnight. He probably had been a hero his whole career, but now the world would know about it. His actions were being broadcast all over the planet, and people would start to see that the world wasn't what it seemed. Charlotte put her other camera down, her attention drawn to the scene unfolding below. A tear pricked her eye as she wondered where the child's parents were.

Everything she had feared was coming to fruition...and the most memorable moment so far had been caught by her camera.

The general huffed and puffed as he pushed hard toward the perimeter. He could see the finish line, but there were so many demons on their back. He twisted around, holding the child close to him as he fired the last of his bullets at the demons.

It wasn't enough.

Just when the general began to think all hope was lost Morris rounded the corner, followed by his team. The general looked at them in the eyes as he ran past with the boy. They were injured and battle-weary, but there was still fight in their eyes.

"General, watch out!"

Morris and his team fanned out to cover the general and the colonel joined them to defend the life of the child in his arms. They fired into the demons, dropping them like dominoes, and the air was choked with their dust. One by one they emptied their clips, until only one demon remained. Brown reached for his knife as it ran at them, but the colonel stopped him.

"Allow me." She smiled and pulled out a short-sword she had strapped to her thigh. She stepped forward and twisted to the right as the demon lunged, and her sword came down swift and hard to sever the demon's head. She stood for a moment breathing heavily and stuck the sword back into its sheath once the blood had turned to dust.

The four guys looked at her for a moment, blinking before nodding in approval and turning to the general. "We gotta get out while we have a break. Come on."

The general headed up the hill with the colonel and the team forming a protective ring around him and the child he carried. The soldiers along the perimeter fired on the demons.

Charlotte shivered as she watched the procession. The sweating general climbed the hill and handed the child over to a female soldier, who quickly took him to the med tent. The boy looked back over her shoulder as she carried him off, keeping his eyes on the general as they went into the tent.

She continued to film as the general paused for a moment outside his mobile command post. He stood with his eyes closed and his face tilted up to the early evening sun.

The clouds in the background framed him in the oranges, purples, and grays of approaching sunset. Charlotte knew she would remember this moment for the rest of her life.

The colonel and the four soldiers ran off to gather more ammo, water, and anything they else they thought they might need before they headed back out. The general took a seat in the grass, smiling his thanks to the soldier who handed him a bottle of water.

Charlotte made her way over to the general, bending down to speak to him before anyone else saw them. "General, I'm Charlotte."

"Yes, the reporter who helped Katie, right?"

"Yes, sir. I was wondering if I might have a word?"

"Of course, but forgive me if I stay planted here in the grass."

Charlotte smiled and sat down next to him. "That was really brave what you just did, getting that little boy to safety. You were a true hero out there."

"All these men and women are heroes, Charlotte. We are all trying to save the world from these crazy demons. No one saw this coming."

"Sir, I thought you might want to know that I overheard some of your men talking about just bombing the entire place."

The general didn't look fazed by the statement. He took a sip of his water and gave her a resigned nod.

"Charlotte, I wish I could tell you the world was a better place; that no matter what we could achieve peace, but that just isn't true—and I think you already know that. To be honest with you, I couldn't argue the tactic. The whole thing would end without any more military casualties. I think, though, that time has come and gone."

The colonel arrived with several magazines for the general. "Sir, I got enough for both of us."

The general groaned and got to his feet and Charlotte followed suit. He sipped his water again and sighed.

"I think I should stay out of the fight and allow you and those four men to take over."

"I understand, sir," the colonel replied. "I am honored that you are allowing me back out."

"I wouldn't have it any other way, Colonel. You are one hell of a soldier."

"Thank you, General."

Charlotte stepped forward and nodded at the colonel, looking at Brushwood. "Sir, if you wouldn't mind, I want to go in and stream the video from the inside. The people of Earth know something is going on, and this is the perfect time to introduce them to the idea that the demons are here and they aren't backing down."

The general sighed as he gazed at the battle. They had been through so much with demons for centuries, and especially in the last few months. He knew it would be a shock, and he also knew that if people weren't told what was going on it would cost many more lives. At the same time, he couldn't make that call. The President was the only person who could.

He went back and forth in his mind and glanced at the colonel, who didn't know what to tell him. Finally he turned back to Charlotte.

"This shit can't stay hidden forever, can it? Those demons are going to find out we humans don't scare so fucking easily! Go. Take a weapon and film whatever you want, but don't get in the way."

"Thank you, sir," Charlotte exclaimed excitedly. "I won't get in the way, and I'll make sure that what I am filming is exactly what the public needs to see."

Charlotte turned to go get a weapon and the general grabbed her arm. "Charlotte, just so you know—this is on *your* head."

Charlotte nodded and ran off to ask one of the soldiers for a gun. The colonel looked at the general and raised an eyebrow; she knew *he* knew it wasn't his choice to make. He looked at her and shook his head.

"Aw, fuck 'em. If they have a problem with it they can take it up with me—*after* I recover from saving their asses."

The colonel chuckled.

Charlotte shoved a clip into her gun as she ran up beside them and nodded at the colonel.

Colonel Jehovivich asked, "You guys ready to kick some more demon ass? Because I am sure as hell ready to get these fuckers and send them straight back to hell. I got a bottle of wine waiting for me at home and I'd rather not wait until it ages."

The guys smiled and Charlotte clicked on her camera again to begin live-streaming as they headed down the hill.

She turned the camera toward her face. "I am heading into the battle zone to film, and I am armed. I will warn you right now: the images on this video will be graphic, so fucking hold onto your hats."

She turned the camera around just as a demon ran up in front of her. She screamed and fired, and Wilson looked at her approvingly as the blood seeped from the demon's head before he turned to dust.

"Shit, kid! Good shot!"

Charlotte chuckled nervously. "Hopefully it's not my last good one for the day."

19

Katie got to the top of the hill and walked next to Eric as they carried him to the med tent. She held his hand tightly as they set him down on the table. The medics quickly surrounded Eric, cutting open his shirt to look at his wound.

Katie leaned down and whispered into his ear, "You'd better make it through, asshole. I'm gonna go whip some more demon ass."

Eric smiled; his teeth were covered in blood. Katie squeezed his hand one more time and turned to leave, wiping her hands on her blood-soaked shirt, but stopped outside the tent and held her stomach. She just needed a minute to gather her composure. She couldn't lose another one. Not like this; not at the hands of *these* assholes.

"Katie?"

She looked up when she heard a familiar voice. "Charlotte? What are *you* doing here?"

Charlotte held up her camera. "Reporter stuff. Why don't you sit for a second and grab some water?

"No, no, I gotta get back to the team." She leaned down and grabbed an armful of water bottles. "But I'm sure they would appreciate it. Hey, stay out of harm's way, okay?"

Charlotte nodded, not really agreeing, but Katie was gone before she could say another word.

Katie tore down the hill as fast as her legs and Pandora could carry her. She didn't slow as she sprinted across the town, plowing straight through four demons standing in her way. She reached the top of the hill and finally began to slow when she saw Joshua and Stephanie take down the last of the ring of demons. There were piles of ash everywhere, and Timothy was sitting on the ground and wiping his head.

"Shit, that was fast."

"Calvin got a little motivated when you ran off with Eric," Korbin explained, nodding at Calvin, who was bent over at the waist trying to catch his breath.

"I grabbed some water for you guys when I was dropping Eric off with the medics." She handed out the bottles, actually glad that she'd grabbed enough to have one herself. She opened the top and guzzled it down, tossing the bottle to the side.

Calvin finished his and walked over to pat her on the shoulder. "Thanks for the water."

Katie nodded and Pandora growled from her throat, "No fucking donuts."

"Sorry, Pandora," Stephanie replied, sticking out her lip. "After the battle, we'll stock up."

Katie laughed. "I keep telling her that."

"And I keep telling *her* they are the fuel that ignites my engine," Pandora replied through Katie.

Everyone laughed for a moment, taking just a second to regroup before they cleared the remaining demons from the nearly-vacant streets. Katie shook her head, knowing the rest of them, including the Enlightened, were hiding in the town, just waiting for their moment to strike. She sure as hell was glad she had done all that training. This battle was far from over.

"How was Eric?" Calvin asked.

Katie shrugged. "Still conscious. I'm sure they will take really good care of him up there."

Pandora cleared Katie's throat. "I also gave his demon a talking-to when Katie was carrying him up the hill. He is going to be working overtime to repair any damage on the inside. The medics might be surprised by how quickly he begins to heal. If not, that demon and I are going to go rounds."

"Thanks, Pandora." Calvin smiled. "You are a lifesaver...literally."

Pandora didn't know what to say; she wasn't used to people thanking her for the things she did. Of course, until Katie, there hadn't been very many humans who would feel a desire to thank her for the pain and evil she had brought into their lives. Only the men thanked her, and that was usually a breathless "thank you" after a good romp in the hay.

The team recuperated for a few more minutes, talking, taking a breather, and regrouping for their next go through the town. They knew it was going to be hard, especially with night approaching, but they couldn't leave until every last demon was killed. The RRF had done an amazing job helping them, as well as the Army. When they finally arrived they had covered the perimeter and sent the remainder of the RRF into the town to start taking out demons.

Pandora had seen more than one battle as they ran through the town, and she couldn't help but notice that it now bothered her. She sighed, watching the team quietly through Katie's eyes. That was when it hit her, and it hit her hard—the team had started to treat her like a *person*, not some slimy demon. They talked to her the same way they talked to Katie, and they appreciated what she did to help the team. There was a swelling inside her that she hadn't felt before, like she was the Grinch at the end of the movie.

Maybe I won't be the scary bitch forever, Pandora thought to herself. *But then again, it's so much damn* fun.

The chair flew across Moloch's office and crashed into the wall, breaking into a hundred pieces. T'Chezz let out a loud growl, clenching his fists and kicking anything and everything he could find. Moloch just sat back behind his desk, sighing as he watched his office's destruction. He had been tired of the furniture anyway, but if T'Chezz went anywhere near his fireplace of souls he would find himself ten floors down with no way to work his way back up.

"They are getting their asses kicked six ways from Sunday. They are a fucking *army*; an army from hell. How hard can it be to kill some fucking humans and take over a few cities?"

"You have to remember, T'Chezz..." He grimaced as a lamp crashed into the wall. "They are low-level idiots without much of a brain. They are stuck on all the food they get to eat."

"There were over a thousand of them. I see...what, maybe five hundred other people down there. They should have broken through already!"

Moloch inspected his claws. "And once they did, what did you really expect? Did you think that they were smart enough to make it to the next city? Please! You are too ambitious, T'Chezz. You are letting your goals cloud the facts. You are unable to see what these beasts are actually capable of."

"More than dying at the hands of those damn mercs!"

"You could have gone down there with them. What you did was send a bunch of idiots into a buffet with no leader to wrangle them. My mercs did their job and secured the town for you. They were not tasked to lead your army."

"I am like any general. I lead from afar, too precious to be put on the front lines."

"Any general but the one fighting your army." Moloch nodded toward the screen playing footage of General Brushwood. The human general carried a child and was shooting demons as down he ran toward the perimeter.

T'Chezz growled and smashed his fists through the top of a table. Moloch rolled his eyes and let out a deep sigh.

"You need to sit down before there are no chairs left to sit on."

T'Chezz glanced at Moloch and took a deep breath. Moloch observed as he mulled over the choices, looked around him, and realized that he had just destroyed Moloch's office. The realization calmed T'Chezz some. He shook his head and wiped his face with his big paws. He went to the armchair in front of Moloch's desk and plopped down, the wood frame creaking under his weight.

Moloch half expected the chair to collapse, which would send him into another temper tantrum, but despite his disappointment at the big-ass demon not landing on the floor and his gratitude at avoiding the tantrum, the chair held. T'Chezz rested his elbows on the arms and steepled his fingers, bringing them up to his chin.

"You may not have gotten the outcome you were hoping for, but you didn't look hard enough here." Moloch clicked on his television and a human newscast appeared on the screen. There were pictures of the battle and video of the demons ripping people apart. "See? You wanted to foment fear, so I would call this a success."

"A *success*?" T'Chezz grumbled, shaking his big head. His eyes were still glowing bright red. "A *success* would be another town taken already, leaving no survivors, and the rest spreading out like my plan entailed. This is just fear. Hell, the damn humans have feared us forever—long before we came to Earth and started taking bodies."

T'Chezz watched the screen, grimacing every time one of his demons turned to dust. They would all be sent to the bowels of hell for this one. Lucifer hadn't known about their plan. He would just see those demons as unlawfully starting a battle and wash his hands of it. He might have gotten on the news, and it might be terrifying the public, but he wanted to do more than that. Earth was *his*, and he was tired of waiting for people to get scared. They would be scared when they watched the demons tear their neighbor limb from limb.

What T'Chezz *really* wanted was to hear them scream for mercy. To have them sign over their souls. To fill hell with the screaming agony of soulless humans for Lucifer to revel in. He wanted to walk the Earth like it was his home, forcing those who were left to do his bidding and watch as the demons slowly destroyed their beloved home. He wanted his sister on a goddamn leash so he could parade her around like a dog for the others to see. He snarled, feeling the irritation building again. He was getting screwed out of everything that he had worked so hard to achieve.

Moloch, on the other hand, rather enjoyed watching T'Chezz so angry, drowning in his own idiotic failure. The time was growing closer; the time to get rid of him once and for all. He could feel it in the pit of his stomach, and when he finally had his way he could go to Lucifer and pin all the chaos on T'Chezz, coming out the hero for destroying him.

It was the perfect plan, and he only hoped he could bring Lilith in as the icing on the cake.

Charlotte, outside the skating rink near the center of town, turned the camera around and looked at her viewers. The number at the bottom of the screen was well over a million by that point, which meant she'd gone viral. Her email count was in the double digits, and she knew other news stations were trying to contact her.

"We have passed through the center of the town, which now lies quiet. There are still hundreds of demons here, and we are looking for them. Some are in hiding, and others are moving from street to street looking for fresh kills. For those of you who think this is some kind of prank, let me remind you that I am on Facebook Live. You are seeing exactly what I am seeing."

A loud bang and several gunshots inside the skating rink caused Charlotte to duck. She turned the camera back around and looked at the colonel and Morris's team, who were reloading their weapons. The double doors out front opened and a demon came flying into the parking lot. It skidded across the cement and stopped right in front of Charlotte, and she attempted to keep the camera steady. The beast had a knife in its skull and its eyes turned to Charlotte for just a moment before it turned to dust.

The colonel chuckled. "You all right there, superstar?"

"Uh-huh?" Charlotte nodded, still in shock.

The four of them crossed the lot and approached the rink's front doors. They peeked inside, where a merc team was fighting a large number of demons. Ella looked at them and smiled for the camera as she sliced through a demon's throat. He wheezed for a moment, wobbling back and forth, so Ella pressed one finger to his chest. He fell backward and turned to dust as he hit the floor.

The New York team was kicking major ass, having stumbled on a huge nest of demons using the skating rink as a hideout. The demons had been listening to bad nineties music as they devoured the employees. The colonel nodded at the Band and they ran in, guns at the ready.

"These are good guys—New York mercenaries. Protect them and they will have your back," the colonel yelled to the Brothers as they jumped the half-wall.

They nodded and laid into the demons, blowing their brains to dust all over the floor. The New York team nodded in thanks as they broke necks. It was a fucking furball of destruction and mayhem —and Charlotte filmed everything.

Ella pranced across the floor and called to one of her teammates, "I wonder if I could do this on roller skates?"

A demon lunged at her and she grabbed it by the neck, snapping her gum and smiling as she drew her arm back to punch it in the face. She threw the demon on the ground and stepped on its neck, examining the scratch it had left on her forearm.

"You fucking dick! I have gone this whole time with no wounds, and here you come with happy fucking claws. Nope! Fuck you."

She pulled her rifle off her back and pulled the trigger, smirking in satisfaction as the bullet blew half of his head away. After he turned to dust she looked at Charlotte and winked, turning back just in time to pull the trigger again —this time taking two demons down at once. She blew on the end of her rifle and smiled.

"That's how you fucking *win* this game, bitches."

Charlotte flipped the camera to her face, the shock of the battle starting to settle in. She stared at the screen for several moments before snapping out of her trance, then sighed and started to talk.

"The battle continues to rage, and I don't know how much battery I have left on this thing, but keep watching. I will keep filming until the phone dies...or I do."

20

Brock groaned. He held his head and rolled over onto his back. His whole face hurt, and he could hear his heartbeat thumping in his ears. That Damned had given it to him *hard*. Slowly he opened his eyes, blinking at the darkening sky. He had been out for hours, and the thought of what had happened to his mother sent panic through him. He tried to sit up but fell back, groaning.

Slow down, beefcake, I only just finished healing you, his succubus snapped. *You have to take it slow for the first few minutes. I know you want to get out there, but if you run into a wall and knock yourself out you'll be no good to anyone.*

You healed me?

Uh, yeah! That's part of my charm. You didn't actually think that pulled hamstring in Virginia healed itself, did you?

Thought maybe I dreamt it.

Brock put his hands down and slowly sat up, pulling his knees up to rest his arms on them. He looked at the lights flickering inside the grocery store, and then around the street. There were bodies, but none that resembled his mother in the flowery dress she wore when she went into town.

What happened while I was out?

Well, there are some good Damned kicking demon ass, the military rolled up, and now it's just a giant shit show. They are battling it out like World War III. Of course, I missed a lot since I was stitching up your fucking brain stem. When you find that fucking dude, let me get a punch or two in.

So if you can fix me, can you do anything else? Like make me fight better, or be stronger? Bigger, even?

Yes, I can do some of that, but I am not a self-help service here. I have to get something in return. I mean, I'm a demon, not your fairy fucking godmother. I can't, however, take you over. You'll never come back, and I don't have the use of my powers like that top side—otherwise you'd have screwed ten dudes by now.

There will be no negotiation about me taking dick! I'll eat a fucking bullet first.

Fine, fine, we will talk later about payback. There's no time for that now. You need to get up and get going. Your mother ran off somewhere out there Rambo-style, so I'm thinking you might find her alive.

Brock stood up and took a deep breath, feeling the succubus-derived strength surge through him. His muscles got bigger and his chest filled out. He turned his neck right and left and the pain in his head subsided.

Shit, where were you when I had hangovers?

Eating fucking humans for lunch.

Why do I even ask? All right, thanks. We'll talk about payback later. Right now I gotta figure out where everyone is and then hunt down that motherfucker who bashed me over the head. There is no way I am going to let him get away with that shit.

Yeah, yeah, the succubus replied.

She pushed Brock's adrenaline, allowing him to run faster across the town, and he looked for demons anytime he turned a corner. She chuckled to herself, knowing that she had just gotten him in a corner. He was going to owe her, and even if she couldn't actually do it, she would threaten to kill him if he didn't give her exactly what she wanted. She liked being back Earth-side, and there was no way she was going to let the fool die, but he didn't need to know that. As far as he was concerned, he had to barter for strength.

I have all the time in the world, she thought to herself. *I'm not giving up on getting some dick until my human is dead and buried. By then I'll be heading back to hell, where there is more than enough demon stuff to satisfy a girl in need.*

The human hostages sat in the back of the bar, staring at the demon mercenaries with anger in their eyes. They had already tried to take the three men out, but that had ended with two dead and one devoured. That had been enough to make them sit still for a little while. At least in there they weren't being chased down by human-eating demons, but they had no idea what these Enlightened had in store for them. It wasn't going to be good, whatever it was.

Brock stuck close to the walls, looking around the town for any signs of human life, and the bright neon lights of the bar blinked on and off almost like a signal. He crept over to the bar and headed around the side to peek into the window. The place was pretty dark, but he could see a group of people huddled together at the back. He scoped out the rest, finding only three demon mercs like the one who bashed him over the head protecting the place. Brock pulled out his knife and flicked it open.

Sure glad Mom got me this for Christmas. Merry Christmas, motherfuckers.

Brock crept around the doorframe and hid behind the counter as the demon mercs paced the floor. One stopped and turned his back to lean against the counter and Brock took a deep breath and stood up, wrapping his hand around the guy's mouth while he drew his knife across his throat. The guy grabbed his neck and dropped his rifle as he fell to the floor, and the second demon whirled and fired as Brock grabbed the dropped weapon and dove under the counter again.

He pressed his back to the counter and clutched the rifle as he strained to pinpoint the other merc's position. Then he heard the soft scrape of a shoe against the linoleum.

He counted to three and jumped up from behind the counter with the rifle at the ready, then pulled the trigger. The bullet spun through the air and hit the demon merc right in the side of the head, sending him flying backward to crash through a bar table. Almost instantly the demon shriveled up, and all that remained was a dead guy on the floor in a pool of blood.

The third merc came around the corner, firing before he even had eyes on Brock. Brock dropped to the floor and fired upward, and the demon jerked and growled as the bullet took him in the shoulder. He continued toward Brock, who scrambled to his feet. The demon fired again and Brock just managed to duck his bullet, which hit the wall inches behind him as he dove into the liquor closet to the side. He grabbed a bottle of whiskey and waited until the demon merc turned the corner, then Brock reared back and hit the demon across the face with it.

The bottle shattered and the demon fell to the ground in a shower of broken glass and whiskey. Brock took his chance—he pinned the demon's chest with his boot, pointed his gun at the demon's head, and smiled. "Bye-bye."

Brock pulled the trigger, but nothing happened.

You have got *to be kidding me*, his succubus moaned.

The demon grabbed his leg and twisted and Brock fell. The merc stood up, pulled a shard of glass from his cheek, and tossed it at Brock. He grabbed his gun and brought it to Brock's head.

"Who's saying bye *now?*"

"You, asshole," a voice shouted from behind them.

Brock covered his head as bullets pelted the demon until his body burst into dust. Brock risked a look into the bar and saw his mother standing there with three other people. All of them were armed, and all of them were angry.

"Don't you *ever* try to harm my boy!"

Brock let out a deep breath and leaned his head against the wall. After all that, his mom ended up saving *his* ass at the last moment. Before that day he would have felt emasculated, but at that moment he didn't give a shit if the Three Blind Mice were standing there as long as the demon was dead and he was alive. Things were definitely getting more interesting by the second.

Everyone was relieved to be rid of those three fuckers, but they had no idea what they needed to do next. Brock had no answers, and his mother was just glad he was alive. She had thought he was dead, and she had made a break for it before the demons killed her too.

"I ended up here in this bar with these people, then those weird demon things came rushing in and we were done. We had no escape. You saved us, really."

Brock held his mother tightly. "No, Mom. *You* saved *me*."

"Can't let those assholes hurt my baby boy again. By the way, you look really well for being bashed over the head. How did you heal so fast?"

"It's a long story, and I'll explain it all later—just as long as no more demons come barreling through the door."

Just then the front doors were kicked open and Korbin stuck his head in. Everyone gasped, stepping back as the three with guns raised them. Korbin grinned at the sight of a room full of non-infected humans.

"*Oh*, a treasure room!" He put his hands up and walked inside. "I am *so* glad to see you all safe and sound. My name is Korbin, and my team is here with me. We have been fighting demons all day. How about we get you people to safety?"

The former hostages let out a collective sigh of relief.

Korbin scanned each person for injuries. He stopped when he met Brock's eyes and a small sigh escaped him, then he moved on to comfort Brock's mother. The people in the bar gathered their things, grabbed whatever weapons were available, and headed over to Korbin.

"We are going to take you all up the hill to the perimeter, where the United States Army is waiting to help anyone who needs it. There is water and medical help there. Just make your way out of here and my team will direct you where to go."

Korbin smiled at each person as they walked out of the bar, and some shook his hand in thanks as they left. It was a nice contrast to the demon-slaying he had been doing all day. He'd expected to find red-eyed bloodthirsty beasts inside enjoying happy hour prices, but instead he'd found a whole bar full of hope. A woman with a floral dress carrying a rifle flashed Korbin a thankful smile as she walked past. Behind her was her kid, the one with the red eyes.

Korbin put his hand out and nodded for Brock to follow him off to the side.

"What's up?" Brock asked.

"Son, I hate to say this, but you are going to have to stay with us."

Korbin led Brock out the front doors and stopped. "I know you just want to get home, but you are Damned—and there are rules."

Brock shook his head in frustration and opened his mouth to argue. He knew what the red in Korbin's eyes meant, but he didn't give a shit. He had been dealing with people like him all damn day. Hell, *he* was like him, but he was not going to get scooped up and sent off somewhere because of the damn succubus inside him.

To his right was a woman kicking the shit out of a demon. He closed his mouth and tilted his head to the side; she was hotter than hell.

"Who is *that*?"

Korbin smiled as he followed the kid's line of sight to Katie. "Oh, she's on my team."

Brock lifted an eyebrow and shrugged, looking back at Korbin. "What the hell, sign me up."

Stephanie slapped Korbin on the back and he laughed at her sassy expression. "Whatever it takes at the moment." He smiled and let out a dry chuckle. "I'm such a pimp."

Stephanie burst into laughter. She covered her mouth with a hand and pounded Korbin on the shoulder. He dropped the smile and pouted.

Stephanie started laughing again. "Aw, it's okay, honey, I think you're the best, even if you are the furthest thing from a pimp I could possibly imagine. I was an *actual* pimp, and let me tell you—it ain't all that shiny."

21

America held its breath as events continued to unfold on their television screens.

Coverage had switched to videos of the Army assisting the people coming out of the town. In the background of the reports, medics flashed a light in each person's eyes to check for the red ring before wrapping a blanket around their shoulders and ushering them through to a protective cordon that had been set up as the battle began to wind down.

News choppers hovered overhead. They were still unable to film the town, but had been allowed to get footage of the cordoned area to show the human victory over the demons to the world.

The general finally lifted the media blackout, feeling that some positive news was needed to reassure the public. He thought Charlotte had done a fantastic job getting down and dirty in the battle, her footage showed the world just how huge a problem they were facing.

However, he also knew humans, and without some positive images to balance the discord of war the public would spiral into fear and panic. Outreaches had already started popping up all over the country, and the churches had opened their doors to those who feared the Revelation was upon them.

The colonel walked up beside the general. "You know, for every person whose fear you calm, five nutjobs will pop up. We are going to have marches all over this country; people saying it's the end of times, not understanding that this war has been going on for centuries."

"Well, with a little education, that will get cleared right up. Mostly. I know I jogged the President's arm on this—and I'm sure I'll hear about it—but it needed to happen. The world has to understand it's no longer a safe place. That we need to bond together to fight for *humanity*, Not for money or oil or any of those other ridiculous things we send our people to war for."

The colonel chuckled. "Why, General, you are starting to sound like a good old down-home hippie. When can I expect you to grow that white hair and beard out?"

"When I retire," he grumped. "Which I am hoping won't be too long."

"Yeah, right. You *live* for this. What would you do after fighting hell's demons—plant a garden?"

"I know what I'm going to do *today* after fighting hell's demons. Well, two things, actually. I am going to hang up my combat helmet and have a fucking drink."

"That drink sounds just about right. I have a feeling there will be a lot of soldiers having drinks tonight—even the mercenary kind—and they all deserve it."

"You seem to have changed your mind about the Damned."

"Not all of them, but I *do* understand that without the merc teams we would have seen a hell of a lot more casualties today. We also would be fighting these damn demons for the next eight years."

"Well, it's not over yet. There are still some down there, and we need to make sure the whole place is clear before we end this. I know everyone is tired, but let's get our battle strategy on and head back out there. And by head back, I mean you and your four superheroes."

"Those boys definitely were worth every penny you had to pay that general to give them to us."

"That was my golfing money."

"You golf?"

"No, but what if I wanted to? Now I can't. I already spent the money."

The colonel laughed and nodded toward the mobile command post. "We should get up there. They want to discuss where we are and where we *need* to be before everyone loses their momentum."

The general nodded and looked at Charlotte, who was dusting off her camera over by the perimeter. She looked exhausted—worn down both mentally and physically—and the general remembered that she wasn't one of the Damned. She didn't have that extra *push* inside her. He frowned and had started to head over when one of the higher-ups from the news station grabbed Charlotte and pushed her toward the town.

"You want to be big time? Then get back out there. This isn't over yet."

"Hey!" the general yelled. "Get your hands off her. Grow a fucking pair, man. We don't allow our civilians to become hell's toys. You want more of a story, you take your pressed-suit ass down there and get it yourself. She's on official military business."

The general put his arm around Charlotte and steered her to the post. He stopped outside and smiled at her. "What an asshole! You okay?"

Charlotte sighed and nodded. "Thanks."

The general shook his head when she let out a huge yawn. "Go get some food and relax. You never know what will happen next."

The general walked into the mobile command post tent and everyone came to attention. He put his hand up and shook his head. "Please, we are all one here. How is it looking?"

His tactical officer put his hands down on the map and looked at it for a second, then ran his finger around the circles the general had drawn before the engagement and nodded. They had been dead on, just like he'd thought.

"We are showing a seventy-percent kill rate for the demons. That means there are still about three hundred of them out there. We closed the circle when the Army got here, and none of them had tried to escape before that point. Now we have fear on our side. They've watched the other demons get mowed down and they are looking for an escape. All of the humans are out of—or coming out of

—the town right now, so they will be in search of fresh meat before long."

"What is your suggestion?"

"I think we should tighten the circle. We need to close it on the center. We push the demons in and keep pushing them. We kill them as we go, and we poke through every inch of this town until we are sure that all the demons are dead."

"I think that's a perfect idea." The general looked at the team leaders, noting their dark-ringed eyes. "We are almost there, fellas, but it's important that we keep ourselves and our teams moving. We need to keep the adrenaline pumping just a little bit longer. This is the time we are most vulnerable. We are worn down mentally and physically and we have let down our guard, even if it's just in our heads. That is when a strike can blindside us. Does everyone have the new loadout of ammunition?"

All the team leaders nodded in the affirmative. The general grabbed his jacket off the chair and pulled it over his blood-stained shirt. He walked over to the map and looked down as he buttoned it down the front.

"Are we downwind?"

"The wind is blowing away from us, sir."

"All right. I want everyone on that side of the perimeter to get their tear gas canisters ready. I want everyone to have their new frag rounds loaded on the Humvees. I want everyone to remember that we have a ton of mercenaries out there and that they cannot be trapped by any of the tear gas. It has the special metal in it, and we *cannot* harm them, even by accident. Is that clear?"

"Yes, sir."

"Good. When the demons start coming out of the woodwork—and they will—I want you to blow them to shit. I don't want there to be enough of a demon soul to go back to hell. I want God to look down from his throne and see one *hell* of a light show down here. Blast those bastards back to where they came from! Is that clear!"

"Yes, sir!"

The team leaders left the post, more energized now than when the general had walked in. He felt the exhaustion; of that, there was no doubt. However, he knew from experience that he had to keep pulling out the energy until everything was over and done with. It was time to end this and send a message to those bastards that the humans weren't going to stand by and let them take their planet and their people.

The mercenaries may have had good deals with their demons, but the rest of them were in for a treat.

The Army was reducing the circumference of the perimeter a little at a time. The humans were still arriving at the top of the hill, where they were checked for red eyes before being sent off to the cordon. This was what the general considered the final stand.

They would not stop until they had squeezed every last demon out of its hiding place and blown their heads right off their damned shoulders.

Across the town, canisters of tear gas were lined up for the taking, although the soldiers were directed to throw it only in safe zones where the mercenaries weren't going to be. After their performance during the battle, none of the soldiers had any question as to where their loyalties lay.

The Humvees rolled up to the perimeter, each carrying the new 30mm fragmentation rounds and a weapons specialist to operate the guns that fired them.

A group of demons emerged from the movie theatre and made a run for the perimeter.

The soldiers stood firm and tossed their tear gas canisters to land about a hundred feet from the approaching demons. The beasts ran right into the fog and clutched helplessly at their throats as the metal incapacitated them. Their wails of pain echoed through the town and they fell to the ground, their senses dulled and their bodies seizing.

Once they were immobilized, the weapons specialists opened fire. The frag rounds exploded and tore the demons apart. Those who were lucky took one to the head and died instantly. Others took a few minutes to crumble to dust, but by that point the soldiers didn't mind watching them suffer in the least.

Across town, a smaller group emerged and zeroed in on the perimeter where the humans were still being processed, but before they even took a step toward the innocents the Army opened fire on them, tearing almost all the demons to shreds before they burst into dust. One, however, managed to dodge the bullets. He leapt over the first line of defense and landed hard on the ground, looking around at the civilians and soldiers with a feral snarl.

The soldiers pulled their weapons, but not fast enough.

The demon lashed out with its claws and hooked a woman by the waist, then tore her body apart even as the soldiers reacted. The demon whirled as it felt the burn of the special bullets in its back and slashed his claws across a soldier's chest, almost cleaving her in two.

Mass panic set in and the civilians scattered, their screams masking the demon's snarls. The soldiers couldn't get a shot off without risking hitting one of the humans. Suddenly a woman tripped, sliding across the grass toward the demon. She scuttled backward and raised her arms over her face, shrieking as the demon picked her up.

"Drop her!" the soldier yelled.

He smirked and bit into her midriff. The soldiers opened fire on the beast and the demon bucked, but continued to tear chunks out of the screaming woman. The general rushed from his tent, pistol at the ready, to see what all the ruckus was about and ran over to the line of soldiers.

"Shoot him in the head! In the *head*!"

The soldiers shifted their aim, but the general pulled the trigger first and his bullet struck the demon right between the eyes. The demon screeched and turned to dust and the body of the woman hit the ground with a thud.

The general turned to the others. "*Always* in the head."

He holstered his weapon and watched the clouds of tear gas drift over the town and away into the distance. The guns had stopped for the moment, but he knew that the tighter they pulled the noose, the more demons would come out of the woodwork.

The general shivered as the chill wind blew over him and looked up as dark clouds rolled across the moonlit sky.

"Something is coming. I can feel it."

22

Moloch paced his office. T'Chezz was on his last nerve.

He repaired the furniture with a wave of his hand as he walked by, gritting his teeth as the furniture moved into place. He was unsure how much more of T'Chezz he could take. Moloch had finally sent him down to get something to eat, which gave him at least ten minutes of peace and quiet.

The war had been a bust, just as he had hoped it would be. The demons had decimated the town, but not a single one of them had made it out. With the military bearing down on them, and the mercenaries in the perimeter working their demon-destroying magic, it wouldn't be long before the entire army was destroyed. T'Chezz was starting to lose it all over again. His incessant whining and tantrums had put a serious dampener on Moloch's mood.

Moloch finished putting the office back together and walked over to the window to look at the lava pits. It was time he made a move; it couldn't wait any longer. He tapped his fingers on the windowsill while he figured out what his next tack should be. He hadn't planned in detail for this, assuming that it would come later rather than sooner. Just then there was a knock on the door and T'Chezz entered before Moloch could answer.

"We are down to less than three hundred demons." He groaned. "This is a disaster, and after Lucifer hears of the failure he will never let me send another army up there. Why did you open that gate if you didn't think it would work?"

"Because you wanted to prove you had earned a place in our ranks. It's not *my* fault the plan failed. I was trying to help you."

"Now I'm completely fucked."

Moloch's eyes blazed red and he turned to face T'Chezz, disgusted to see a tuft of hair from his lunch clinging to his chin. Moloch grimaced at the sight, wanting nothing more than to pull him limb from limb, and he marched forward, stopping just inches away. He growled and his lip curled as he created a portal, then grabbed T'Chezz by the neck and pushed him through.

"Stop leading from behind like a sniveling wimp! Go meet the one you tricked. I'm sure she has a few words for you! And for *fuck's* sake, wipe your dinner off your chin!"

With that he slammed the portal closed and leaned against the desk, letting out a deep breath. The office was blissfully silent, and T'Chezz was out of his hair for good. He knew T'Chezz stood no chance against his sister or the other droves of mercenaries ready to take his head.

"Finally, peace and quiet," Moloch sighed.

A laugh filled the air as Baal appeared in his office. "How did that feel?"

Moloch jumped, putting his large black paw against his chest and breathing deeply. Was there no such thing as privacy down here? He sat down behind the desk and leaned back, then lifted his clawed feet onto the desk and put his arms behind his head.

"Damned good. I've wanted to do that for so damned long!"

"What if Lilith doesn't kill him?"

"Oh, I'm sure she will, but if not, I have a special level of hell all mapped out for him when he returns. He will be buried so deep that Lucifer will forget he ever existed. The rest of us will breathe a sigh of relief, knowing the asshole will be quiet for a few hundred years."

Baal flopped down in the armchair in front of Moloch's desk—and the legs gave out and Baal crashed to the floor. Moloch put his feet down and leaned forward.

Baal laughed and got up. He brushed himself down and popped a puppy he pulled from his pocket into his mouth.

"I just fixed that fucking thing."

"Obviously not well enough." Baal chuckled. "You really should do something with this ceiling. The lava doesn't go with your motif."

"You've been watching human television again, haven't you?"

Baal looked up at him and shrugged. "They all look so delicious."

T'Chezz looked around. He had landed in the town he had sent his demons to. He pulled the fur from his chin, throwing it to the ground. He was enraged; his fists were clenched, his teeth bared. Moloch had tricked him; set him up only to push him through a portal to Earth, just like T'Chezz had done to Lilith when he had wanted her out of the picture.

He growled loudly and punched the side of the building. Stone crumbled to the ground as he stepped into the abandoned street.

He looked up at the hill where the soldiers were stationed. The humans milled around like ants, not knowing yet that he had arrived. Slowly his fists began to unclench and a smile moved over his lips.

"Maybe this isn't as bad as I thought. Maybe this is *exactly* where I need to be to show these humans who the master of Earth really is." T'Chezz let out a deep laugh, which was interrupted by gunfire behind him.

Slowly he turned around, tilting his head to look at the men in uniform aiming their weapons at him. He batted away the bullets coming toward him and took several large steps before backhanding the soldiers. They flew to the right and left, their bodies hitting the ground in a series of thuds. He chuckled as more military rolled toward him and turned as the mercenaries ran out to save the day.

The mercs attempted to fire their weapons at him, but the bullets only hit his thick skin and fell to the ground. They took a step back, watching as T'Chezz smiled and picked up one of the soldiers and chomped down on him. They could hear his bones crack and break as he chewed him up and spat out the skull.

Their weapons didn't work on him, but he wasn't big enough to target with their larger ones. It was a bad situation all around, and no one really knew what to do at that point. They threw knives, swords, and fired weapon after weapon, only for T'Chezz to race forward and attempt to kill more of them.

T'Chezz's growls and roars were audible on the hill. The general stepped back out of his tent and looked around, trying to pinpoint the source of the sounds. He noticed a group of soldiers peering down into the town and pushed them aside, seeing a very large demon—one that hadn't been there before, or at least not that anyone there had noticed. He was too big to hide, but too small to aim at with the Humvees. The general tightened his jaw and marched back into the tent.

"Sir, what is it?" his tactical officer asked.

"A very big fucking problem is what it is. I want you to radio the teams at the C-17s. Tell them to unload the Stryker and just have them stand by. I don't know where this demon came from, but I don't want to wait around to find out if there are more of him."

"Yes, sir."

Down in the town more and more mercs came out of the buildings they'd been searching and edged closer; close enough to get a full view of T'Chezz. None of them had seen a demon that powerful and strong before, and they knew there was no way that they were going to be able to take him.

T'Chezz found the whole situation amusing. They had been Big Billy Badasses when it came to demolishing his army, but now that *he* was there they just froze or ran off to safety.

"Stupid humans," he grumbled. He wondered where his beloved sister was. "Don't worry, I will have each and every one of you as a snack before the night is over with. Go on, run away! Tell your general. Tell your mercenary leader. Tell whoever you want that T'Chezz has arrived and shit is about to get crazy. I rule this turf now, and you will all answer to me."

He growled as the clouds continued to darken overhead. This had not been in the plans.

Katie crept through the old farmhouse on the outskirts of town. She didn't sense any demons near, but she still didn't trust that instinct fully. She could have sworn she'd seen someone in the window as they passed, and she wanted to make sure there were no more innocents left in or near the town. As she crept up the steps, the hair stood up on the back of her neck.

Pandora chuckled. *What's wrong with you?*

I don't know. I guess old houses just creep me out.

Why? You afraid there's a ghost in here?

I think I would welcome a ghost after the things I've seen. If I were human I would need therapy.

You probably still do.

Ha, ha, very... Wait, did you hear that?

Katie froze on the staircase and listened hard. There it was again—the whimper of a child. Katie took off up the stairs, fearful that a child was in danger. She headed down the hall and burst through the only closed door in the house—and came to a stop when she saw a mother, father, and two small children huddled in the corner of the room. They all looked like they would never be the same again. Katie put her weapon away and held out her hand toward them.

"Hey," she began kindly. "My name is Katie, and I am one of the good guys. I am here to get you guys to safety. Outside, up on the hill, are a whole lot of Army soldiers, and they have a safe place for you to go. Will you come with me?"

The father and the mother looked at each other for a moment and back at Katie. The father finally nodded and they picked up their children, and Katie sighed in relief. When the little girl looked at her curiously Pandora did her best to keep the red out of Katie's eyes, knowing it would scare the hell out of these poor humans. They must have hidden there for the whole day, listening to the terrifying sounds of the demons tearing their town apart around them. Neither Pandora nor Katie knew how the family had been lucky enough to not be found, but all that was important at that point was getting them to safety.

The mother smiled at Katie and let her lead them back down the stairs. As they walked out of the front door and onto the porch Katie groaned and grabbed her chest. It was like the burning before—only magnified by a thousand. There was something huge close by; she could feel it.

The woman stepped forward and put her hand on Katie's shoulder, only to pull it back in shock at the sight of Katie's bright red eyes. She couldn't control it; whatever caused the burning made her eyes shine brightly as well.

"I'm sorry, I don't mean to scare you. I *promise* I am one of the good guys," Katie told the mother to calm her nerves. She looked at her curiously for a moment, then followed Katie's stare behind them to where three armed military men were heading toward them. "You see those men coming toward us? They are Army soldiers. Go to them. They will get you to safety."

They ran off the porch and Katie bent at the waist, almost doubled over as she gripped her chest in pain. She gasped for breath, looking into the distance with watery eyes. A loud growl echoed through the valley, sending chills down Katie's spine. She had never felt anything like that before.

Pandora, what's going on?

He's here, she hissed.

Who is here?

T'Chezz. You better let me take over your body.

Katie nodded and took a deep breath to prepare for the switch. Pandora pushed her way through Katie and took her over. Her body morphed, her breasts growing larger, her waist smaller, and her hips wider. Her hair darkened and lengthened by several inches. When the change was done Pandora stood on the porch staring toward the center of town.

"I've got this," Pandora announced aloud. "It's time Earth realizes Mother is here to protect it."

23

Pandora growled as she stepped out of the alley. T'Chezz stopped torturing the people around him for a moment and dropped the body in his hand. A malicious grin split his features as he stepped forward to greet Pandora.

"Well, well, well," Pandora snarked. "Look what the cat dragged in."

T'Chezz looked down his nose at her. "Ah, Lilith. Or is it 'Pandora' these days? Or maybe you go by your human's name now, since you have become her slave?"

Pandora sneered. "Do I *look* like a slave?" She gave her brother a condescending look as she ran a hand down her body. "Nope, definitely *all* me. Seems you are mistaken about how things work up here. Then again, you were *always* slow on the uptake."

T'Chezz gritted his teeth. He had forgotten how much of a bitch his sister could be. "Enough small talk. Time for you to go back home."

Pandora growled. "You'll have to kill me first."

T'Chezz lunged at her and swung. "That can be arranged."

Pandora leapt to the side and struck T'Chezz on the arm, snapping the bone in half. He growled loudly and switched stance, favoring his good arm to give his body a chance to heal the bone while he continued to fight. Pandora smirked and slid across the blacktop. She grabbed T'Chezz by the shoulders and used him as a fulcrum as she kicked his kneecap out. The leg bent inward and the knee popped out of its joint. He screamed and reached down with his good arm to pop it back in. His other arm was almost healed again.

She picked up a car from the street and threw it toward him, but he knocked it to the side as he charged her. She laughed loudly and waited until the last second, then she jumped and punched his arm again to break the bones in the same place. She knew if she kept him healing he wouldn't be able to fight as hard.

"Just like when we were younger; always with your tactics." He laughed and picked up a car, flinging it at her as she landed.

The car hit Pandora hard, sending her flying to land on her back across the street. She got up, shook it off, and tore down the street after him. Nobody would ever question just how strong she was again after she grabbed a truck with one hand and slung it at her brother. It hit T'Chezz in the chest and he staggered and groaned, but he recovered quickly and clamped his healed arm around the truck, crushing it into a ball.

Pandora grimaced, narrowing her eyes. He threw the

ball of metal and she dodged to the side, but not far enough. The ball hit her in the shoulder, and she sprawled to the ground. She laid there a minute, then sat up, clapping her hands.

T'Chezz growled at her snarky response, hating her even more on Earth than he ever had in hell.

Pandora got to her feet and shook her head. "You had one chance to kill me, but fortunately for me you are a complete fuck up. I was inserted into a Nephilim!"

T'Chezz took an involuntary step back with a look of shock on his face. "There aren't any of those left!"

Pandora shrugged her shoulders, sending a motorcycling spiraling toward his head. "Guess I'm wrong, then. Maybe she's just a normal human who can kick ass. Either way, you are *fucked*!"

Moloch was sitting back in his office chair with a popcorn bucket full of kittens on his lap, munching away as he watched the fight between Pandora and T'Chezz. He couldn't stop laughing at how badly T'Chezz was getting beaten. He picked up a kitten and it wiggled free, then jumped to the ground and ran off.

"Damn it, I hate when that happens. I'll end up finding it under the couch, all decomposed. A shame; these are my favorite."

Moloch shrugged and went back to the entertainment, almost spitting a kitten out when a motorcycle hit T'Chezz in the head and knocked him off his feet. Just seeing the look on his face made every part of his plan worth it. Still, there was something strange about the way they were fighting; something different than normal. Moloch's laugh began to fade and he slowly sat up, narrowing his eyes. There was no sound, so he couldn't hear what they were saying.

"How can she use so much of her power on Earth?"

Pandora stepped back and put her hands on her knees while she caught her breath. She might look like her human form, but she was still using Katie's organs and her lungs definitely needed a workout or two. She had just stood up, ready to go again, when T'Chezz stood up tall and straight and put his arms out to both sides, pulling his energy inward. Pandora watched unamused as T'Chezz grew larger and larger until he towered over her. He looked down and let out a deep bellowing laugh.

"I knew if I grew larger I could take you out in a heartbeat. I also knew that you couldn't grow larger without destroying the human you're in, which obviously you won't do. You have been brainwashed."

"If I have," Pandora yelled, "then it's your fucking fault for sending me back here in the first place."

"Get off it. We all know you were planning on leaving anyway."

"On my own terms, T'Chezz. You don't rule me, and last time I checked I was much higher than you on the food chain. Hell, at this point, after the mess you have made, *dog shit* will be higher on the fucking food chain than you."

"Enough!" T'Chezz screamed, rattling the windows around them. He stomped forward with his fists clenched.

Pandora put her hands on her hips and lifted an eyebrow. "You are now officially the world's largest dumb-ass. They can put you in the record books."

"Funny how you joke when I am about to send you and your human spiraling back to hell."

I hear hell's a little warm this time of year, Katie remarked in Pandora's mind.

Honey, it's hot all *the time.*

Katie chuckled and brought Pandora's attention to the field behind T'Chezz. *There...that should do the trick.*

Very nice, human. Very nice.

Pandora cleared her throat and put her hands to her mouth, yelling up at T'Chezz, "Ask not for whom the bells toll, motherfucker. It tolls for *you!*"

With that she leapt to the side, shielding herself from what was to come. The sound of the Stryker drew T'Chezz's attention to the field and he growled when they began to shoot at him, blowing massive chunks out of his body. He screamed as he twisted back around to Pandora.

Pandora smiled sweetly and pointed upward, where several attack helos hovered.

The pilot smiled as he pressed the button to send a steady stream of the special bullets at his head.

T'Chezz ducked, but a round hit him in the back. His head and arms jerked backward, exposing his chest and neck. The helo pilot aimed the gun and held the button down, and the bullets ripped into the demon's muscular neck. Pandora peeked over the wall she was hiding behind and smiled as her brother and worst enemy was blown to bits by the very military he had spent so much time mocking.

Pandora stood up amongst the gunfire and explosions and clapped slowly.

"Congratulations, brother. Not only was your demon army a complete failure, you also came up here talking a big game only for the *real* military to blow your head clean off your shoulders. You really should get a new hobby, because world domination seems to be just a *little* bit beyond your capabilities. Maybe you could take up knitting? I'm sure my husband would *love* a handmade afghan for his fire couch at home. Then again, you would probably fail at that too and end up knitting him a cross or something equally ridiculous. You should probably just let them kill you. Oh wait, you don't have a choice anymore, do you?"

She laughed, ducking back behind the stones to watch as the red flickered in T'Chezz's eyes. The bullets tore through his last layer of skin and his head fell from his body and rolled to a bumpy stop farther down the street. T'Chezz was gone, and after all that time fretting, it had been easier than she had thought it would be.

Pandora stood up again and, hands on her hips, gave her body back to Katie.

Katie laughed. *That's a really big fucking head.*

I heard he overcompensated.

<hr />

The Army moved forward, the soldiers attacking the demons' flanks to force them into the center of the town.

Gunfire raged as the soldiers advanced, intent on taking down as many of the demons as they could in a short period of time. After T'Chezz was killed the soldiers had gotten their mojo back. Morale boosted, they found the strength to push through and take out every last demon in the entire town. The demons didn't know which way to turn, and left with no option, they went to ground—which for them meant straight back to hell.

They needed to hide from the destruction the Army was bringing down on them. There was no more standing around at the perimeter. The soldiers meant business. Strykers rumbled through the streets as helicopters decimated buildings from the sky, taking out droves of demons with a single strike. The mercs sat watching from the hill above, their end of things done. The town might not have been saved, but some of the people had—which made it all worthwhile to them.

The teams knew that sending a demon back to hell didn't mean you would never see it again, but they were doing the best they could with what they had been given. The attack had come out of nowhere, an offensive by the demons' upper echelon to get a foothold on Earth and humanity. From the soldiers and mercenaries to the reporters and bystanders, no one had been willing to stand by and allow that to happen. Not to their planet, and *especially* not to their people.

Ella leaned her head against Katie's shoulder and yawned. Katie chuckled, exhausted from letting Pandora take over. Ella looked at the chipped polish on her nails.

"I think I'm gonna start fighting in gloves."

"Like white-gentleman gloves, or like winter gloves?

Because it would be funny as hell if you slapped a demon with one of your white gloves."

"A duel!" Ella raised her fist into the air, laughing.

Katie patted her on the leg and returned to watching the town. The Humvees and Strykers had backed the last remaining demons into the town square and the soldiers surrounded them, pausing for a moment before they unleashed their weapons. The screeches of the final ten demons echoed briefly before cutting out as the demons turned to dust.

Then there was silence.

No birds chirped, no demons or humans screamed. The guns were at rest in the soldier's hands. All of the humans silently processed their losses, and the teams bowed their heads, thinking of the innocents who lost their lives.

The fight had been a long one, starting with a crash and ending with almost total destruction. Katie had heard that the soldiers had at first talked about dropping bombs on the place, but as her gaze roved across the townspeople they'd saved Katie was really glad that movement hadn't been authorized.

Calvin walked over and nodded to Katie as he sat down beside her. "You know, there was a point during this fight where I thought we were gonna lose."

Katie looked at Calvin. "There's a moment in every battle where that thought crosses our minds. It almost poisons us while we fight for our freedom and the lives of every innocent person out there. But what is most important is that we don't buckle under that fear. We don't let it get to us so badly that it ends up being the last fight."

"Thank Pandora for us for taking out T'Chezz. I know

he was one of your biggest threats, and from how big he got we were lucky he decided to show up here. I don't know if we would have been able to control him."

You are welcome, big man.

"She says you're welcome," Katie smiled as the exhaustion flooded her body. "We are both a bit tired from what happened."

"Did you remember anything this time?" Damian asked. He was sitting on the other side of Calvin.

"Yeah, actually I saw the whole thing through Pandora's eyes. I couldn't control anything, but I saw it. Oddly enough, it wasn't even the most terrifying part of the day. We lost so many innocents. But now the demons know that fucking with us can only end one way."

O n the hills above the small Wyoming town, the stains left by the wounded and dead dulled the rippling green grasses. Anchors were still stuck in the ground where the mobile command post had stood, and the tires on the large military machines ravaged the virgin grasses as they moved slowly back to the C-17s parked in the fields beyond. The cries of the wounded could be heard all over, and the walls of the white med tent were spattered with blood.

The blood of the wounded, the blood of the dead, and the blood of those who wished they *had* died.

The town was empty, covered in dust, soot, and blood and stained by the echoes of the screams that had filled the streets just hours before. All along the roads, bits and pieces of bodies lay where they'd been dropped.

A crumpled cell phone lay on the sidewalk, the screen frozen forever on its final call to 911. A boy's body lay askew beside it, his dark hair fluttering in the breeze as one hand reached out for the phone.

The fountain in the center of the town was blocked, the basin filled with effluvia from the bodies dropped into the water by the demons. A thick layer of demon dust coated the steps to the town hall, now silent and empty.

The abandoned buildings were left open and unlocked, the bulbs flickering in their fixtures. The houses should have been full of life and laughter, yet there were no families smiling and laughing over dinner, no children playing in their front yards, and no animals roaming the lush pastures. The church bell lay on its side in the street beside a huge piece of paving its impact uprooted when it fell from the steeple. There was no joyous praise to God coming from that stained-glass building on that day.

Maybe not on any other day after this, either.

The survivors were already talking about leaving. No amount of bleach and scrubbing could purge the memories from their heads. Many had watched the people they loved die and they were confused as to why they were still alive —and confused as to why the demons had chosen their town to wreak their havoc. They were simple people; never loud, never flashy and always community-minded.

Even with their town half-destroyed and covered in demon dust, the people checked on their neighbors—their neighbors being the ones in the cot or gurney next to them.

The playground was silent, the swings gently blowing in the breeze. There were no children near to use it. The school had been evacuated, leaving papers in the halls, basketballs on the gym floor, and the television still playing in the history classroom where they watched the news every afternoon.

On the screen were pictures of the vacant town. The newscaster looked sorrowful as she asked viewers where *they* would hide when the horror finally made it to their town. The ticker running along at the bottom of the screen read, "Incursion day: the start of the War of the Damned."

Those from that small Wyoming town knew the war had already begun, leaving a hole in their town and in their lives. They'd had a gruesome taste of what hell could unleash in the war to come.

Even beyond the town limits, the impact of the demon incursion could be felt. Lives had been taken, souls had been touched, and the children of that town would never again be innocent.

Death changed everything, and it had changed the survivors from the moment the first life had been taken. The memory of the fallen would forever rest in the grasses and gravel of the town's quiet little streets.

Brock sat on the grass on top of the hill, as far from the cordoned area where his mother was that he could get. He already knew that being Damned meant he would never see her again, but he didn't know the extent of it until Calvin walked over. He sat down next to the rock star and let out a long deep breath.

"You doing all right?"

"Yeah. No... I guess I'm just waiting for someone to explain to me what all of this means."

Calvin chuckled and looked out over the silent town. "Being Damned is an interesting experience. Some love it, some hate it, and some just live their lives the best that they can."

"Can I tell people?"

"No. In fact, from today forward everyone will think that you died. Your ashes will be presented to your family, and an excuse will be made for what happened to you. You will be declared legally dead, so you won't have a license, bank account, or anything else that could attach you to this world. We will give you a chance to take care of your finances, move money, and take money out before it is announced, but after that..." He mimed the action with his hand. "Poof."

"No more band. No more traveling, no more chicks, no more rock and roll."

"I'm afraid not." Calvin shrugged. "The Straights will need a new lead singer, my friend."

"Then what? If I'm dead, what can I do?"

"You have three choices as a Damned. You can become research, you can die for real, or you can join us and fight. We are an elite force of mercenaries. We live on a base outside Las Vegas, train, laugh, do things as a family, and fight the demons that attack."

"That may be my only option. I definitely don't want to be a human pin cushion, and I'm not ready to die." He shrugged. "I guess if you guys can do it, I can too."

"I'm sorry this life chose you, man, but you will find good people. And you *will* have a life. It'll just be different than you imagined."

"Can I trade demons?"

Calvin lifted an eyebrow and looked at him. "Trade? You mean like get an upgrade? No."

"Fuck," he mumbled. "My demon is a succubus and I'm a straight guy. A *very* straight guy."

Calvin covered his mouth to hide a chuckle.

"It's really not funny! This thing constantly wants men. She never talks about anything else."

"I'm not laughing at you, it's just comical to me because out tech guy is a gay male who has an incubus who's constantly trying to get him to sleep with women. If you could trade it would actually be perfect, but you can't, sooo..."

"So become gay or live with the horror in my head?"

Calvin struggled to hold back his laughter back and make the guy feel better, but it was really hard. "Most of the time your demon can be controlled. Sometimes they will begin to work *with* you instead of against you, and sometimes they can just be straight suppressed. Try not to think about it too much, and when we get you back to base we can have Katie and Pandora do a once-over on your demon."

"I know who Katie is, but who is Pandora?"

"Pandora is Katie's demon."

"Wait, so the chick who fought the big fucker—she is the same chick as Katie?"

"Yeah." Calvin smiled. "I know, it's confusing. It's confusing to us, too. We don't have the powers Katie and Pandora have. They are two very badass women, and they know it."

"All this is so weird." Brock lay back in the grass and rubbed his face. "It's like going to sleep and waking up the next day to find out Twilight and sparkling vampires are real. It just sounds so crazy, but here I am—and I know my demon is real. She doesn't know when to shut the hell up most of the time. Oddly, she is pretty quiet right now."

"You'll find that most demons tend to hide when Katie comes around. There is something about Pandora that none of them wants to face."

Korbin and Stephanie hung out together on the hill while the rest of the team relaxed and recouped. Korbin had his arm wrapped around Stephanie's shoulders and they had a blanket from the med tent pulled up over their laps. Katie watched from a distance as Stephanie tilted her head toward Korbin's, closing her eyes as he kissed her softly. An aura of love surrounded the two of them.

Katie smiled. They were off in their own little world for the moment.

Katie couldn't shake her anger. She hated that their moment would be over too soon, and she was pissed at everything she had been forced to put off for so long. Everyone was just stuck in their lives, stopped in time by an accident or fluke event. The whole team had lost their futures, and while everyone sort of felt that way after an event like this, the Damned were the ones who had to slink back into the shadows and hope to survive another day.

It was frustrating to Katie because there wasn't a thing she could do to change it.

Damian walked up to Katie and followed her eyes to

where Korbin and Stephanie snuggled together in the grass. 'Shame we can't..."

Damian watched as Katie's eyes narrowed, flashes of red coming from them. She looked at him for a moment. "Sometimes Damian, choices about what is right or wrong are taken from you."

She started to walk across the grass toward Korbin and Stephanie, Damian shaking his head and calling out as he trailed behind her. "Katie, what are you going to do?"

Katie smiled and kept going, ignoring his question. She was going to do something good for people she loved.

Because she couldn't keep waiting; couldn't spend her life afraid that one of them wouldn't make it home after a battle like today's. They had something very few Damned had ever tasted, and that was love.

She wasn't going to let them waste it in the shadows.

Korbin and Stephanie looked up at Katie with a smile. "You okay?" Korbin asked.

Katie nodded. "Let me ask you a question. Would you two like to enjoy your life together?" Katie opened her hands wide and looked around them. "Get married? *Live...* without all of this?"

Stephanie lifted her head from Korbin's chest. "Of course."

Korbin smiled and kissed the top of her head. "Without a doubt."

Neither of them saw through the question or realized what Katie was asking them. For that reason alone, Katie knew it was the right choice. They had just given her permission to pull their demons out of them.

Katie looked behind her as Damian motioned for the

others. They walked up behind Katie as she said her final words to Stephanie and Korbin.

"I love you both. Live happily ever after for me, okay?"

Before they could respond Katie bent down and Pandora pulled the demons out of them both at the exact same time. Their demons hissed and growled impotently as Pandora cast them back to the depths of hell. Both Korbin and Stephanie passed out, falling into each other. The team cheered and Calvin and Damian came to stand beside Katie and pat her on the shoulder. They all loved those two so much that they were willing to let them go so they could have a future.

"I am gonna leave the rest up to you, Damian."

"I can handle that."

Calvin hugged Katie tightly. "You know he'd have kicked your ass if he'd understood what you were about to do, right?"

"I'm not letting true love die because of this war, Calvin."

Calvin smiled and put his arm around her shoulder as they walked away, leaving Damian with their former team-mates. "Hey, I agree, and for what it's worth I'm voting for what you did."

"I guess it's a good thing he won't remember," she replied as Calvin chuckled. They looked at the two of them one last time. "I'm just glad *I* will. Those two made a huge impression on my life, and right or wrong I will miss the hell out of them."

The general stared across at the table at Katie. They had been brought back to the base for a debriefing, and to give Eric the best care he could get. It wasn't home, but they were getting closer. Though they had only been gone for a couple of days, Katie really missed the base and the quiet of her mountainside workout space.

"Katie, first I want to say that I think what you did for Korbin and Stephanie was really good of you. We will make sure they get set up and want for nothing."

"Thank you, General."

"As far as the rest of it, I wish I could tell you what to expect. We are now at war—not that we haven't been for a long time, but now it's official. This war will change the rules. It will push humanity to its limits, and force us to make decisions that would otherwise seem completely out of the question. In reality I have no idea what it will all mean for us, but we are working hard to avoid any more major surprises."

Katie chuckled. "Good luck with that."

The general gave her a wry smile. "I suspect the demons will wait a bit before opening a portal of that size again, but the politics of it all are going to start heating up. I don't even know what to expect here from my position. What I *do* know is that *you* are not in the safest position. None of the Damned mercenaries are. I want you and your team, and the other teams for that matter, to stay as hidden as you can for now. I want there to be a long and prosperous future between us, and I promise that includes your business."

Katie let out her breath and smiled at the general. "Thank you, General. I appreciate your concern. We have definitely come a long way since the first time I contacted you, that's for sure. I never thought I would be fighting alongside the military, but I have to admit your men were invaluable to us during the fight. They really held their own, and I want to say that we all mourn the loss of the police officers and soldiers who were killed in the battle."

"I appreciate that, and we will be keeping Eric in our thoughts and prayers as well. Life has a funny way of forcing people together and showing them the right path—even when they try to resist."

The general stood up. Katie followed suit and accepted his outstretched hand. They were parting as friends, not just business associates or war partners, but actual friends. That made Katie feel a lot more at ease about the secrecy and the future of the mercenaries. She left the room and made her way to the sick bay where Eric was being cared for. She stood in the doorway to his room for several moments, watching his chest rise and fall, the sound of the heart monitor echoing through her ears. He looked so quiet and peaceful, yet she knew he had spent the last day fighting for his life.

Eric was healing now and in the clear, but it had been a long wait to know he was going to be okay. They were going to allow him to be transported to their base under their care the next day, so everyone was looking forward to that. Katie walked into the room and stood by the bed, looking down at him.

He's going to be okay, right?

Yes, but his demon is too weak, Katie. He'll heal, but it's only time at this point. The demon cannot do anything else to speed it along.

Katie nodded, then closed her eyes. *Fuck it.*

She opened her eyes as her hand passed into Eric's chest. She grabbed Eric's demon and ripped it out of him, casting it back to hell with ease. The demon was so weak it didn't even attempt to fight back.

Pandora laughed. *Well, that's new.*

———

The team waited another day at the general's base to ensure Eric was ready for transport. He was still unconscious, and they weren't sure if his exorcism had taken his memories or if he would still be the same guy who had joined the team with no demon not long before. All they cared about at that point, though, was making sure he was all right after the injuries that he had sustained.

Once they were back at the base, Calvin instructed everyone to take a couple of days to get back into their daily routine and recover from the trauma of the incursion. That battle had been the most trying action they had ever seen. The things they'd seen would be forever burned into their memories. The team was used to traumatic things, but it took some time to get back to whatever passed for normal with them.

Katie spent her two days between training on the hill, sleeping, eating a massive number of donuts, and watching soap reruns. Timothy had originally locked himself in the ops room, but after a day alone he came back out to be around everyone else. He missed Stephanie and Korbin; they all did. None of them felt at home without them there. But by the next day, the team was ready to sit down and talk about the future.

They met around the large wooden table in the conference room and everyone looked at Calvin. He had been the number two, which automatically made Korbin's seat his. No one had any qualms about that—no one but Calvin.

He stood up from the table and cleared his throat. "I've been thinking about this a lot, and I have been the number two for a long time. I made a really fantastic second behind Korbin, and when I think about moving from that spot it just doesn't feel right. It doesn't feel like the natural course of action for me or for the team. I would like to suggest that we move Katie into Korbin's place, and I'll do what I do best."

It went around the table. Everyone including Damian more than agreed that it was the perfect place for Katie. She was taken aback by it, not expecting it at all, but she agreed to accept. She was proud to walk in Korbin's shoes and sit in the place where her friend and mentor once had.

Korbin had helped her become who she was as a demon hunter, and his influence had shaped her as a person as she adjusted to her new life.

"Thank you, guys. I hope that over time I can learn to lead this team as well as Korbin did."

"So...because you are the new leader, you get to choose a new name." Damian smiled.

Katie thought about it for a moment, running through different options in her head. "I want to keep Killers, so how about we just do 'Katie's Killers?'"

"I like that," Joshua agreed with a smile.

"Me too," Timothy replied, giving the thumbs-up.

"We are now Katie's Killers, and may the team continue!" Calvin pronounced triumphantly.

Katie leaned back in her chair and looked at the faces of her family. They were entering a new era for demon hunters. There was a new war, a new leader, and a new attitude toward the way the world was changing. Katie hoped that with the politics came a renewed sense of camaraderie between the mercs and the military. She had worked hard to cement that relationship, and she hoped public knowledge of demons didn't change it.

All she could do was sit back and wait.

Katie got up from the table and walked over to the counter, picking up a box of donuts and setting it down in the middle of the table. Pandora spoke through Katie's throat to the group.

"To a new and bright future."

"To Pandora!" Calvin cheered, grabbing a donut and holding it in the air.

Pandora snickered. "Don't get all mushy on me now, big man."

On the other side of the state on a long dirt road in a mountain valley with alfalfa fields on both sides was a small farmhouse. It had bright red shutters, a wraparound porch, and a swing out front. The garden was huge, with rows and rows of flowers and vegetables growing strong in the warm sun. It was early in the afternoon in on a perfect spring day, and a woman walked out onto the porch in a pair of shorts and a t-shirt. She stretched her arms over her head and let the sun beat down on her face.

A pair of arms wrapped around her waist and squeezed. "Korbin!"

Korbin lowered his head and kissed Stephanie sweetly on the cheek, taking in the fresh scent of her lavender shampoo. "That was a good afternoon nap."

"Yes, it was." She smiled and turned to wrap her arms around his neck. "You ready to get some gardening done? We should have some veggies ready to harvest."

Korbin cupped her chin in his hand and kissed the tip of her nose. "Sure."

"I'm just gonna grab my gardening gloves."

Korbin nodded and let go, swatting Stephanie on the butt as she passed. He walked down the steps into the yard, staring out in appreciation at fields. Stephanie snuck up behind him, giggling as she leapt onto his back. He laughed as he fell over his tangled feet, taking her down into the grass with him. He rolled over on top of her and stared down into her beautiful blue eyes.

"This is the perfect place for us."

"I know." Stephanie smiled. "I still can't believe that after all those years in that awful apartment, that guy just showed up and offered cash for that useless old base that I owned. What was his name?"

"Uh, Damian, I think."

"Yes, that's it. Well, I think that it turned out splendidly for us. I couldn't imagine a more perfect life than this."

"Me either." Korbin smiled, looking up at the sound of a bark.

He rolled over and sat up in the grass as a black and white dog came barreling off the porch. The dog tackled Korbin and licked him all over his face. The laughter from the two of them echoed across the land.

In the distance, Katie stood watching the two of them. She was finally at peace, knowing they couldn't be any happier. That was all she had wanted for them: a life together, with love and a chance to have the family they both wanted but had never thought was possible. A chance to be more than demon hunters.

Korbin and Stephanie both had done so much for other people throughout their entire lives, and they deserved every ounce of happiness they could get. Damian had set it up, since he knew exactly what they would need to make their lives perfect from conversations they'd had while they were on the base. Part of Katie was envious, but the other part knew she had a long fight ahead of her before she could even consider her own dreams.

Until that day she would be strong and do whatever it took to win the war.

Katie pulled her hood over her head, sending her love to Korbin and Stephanie one last time even if they didn't know who she was anymore. "I promise I will fucking kill every last demon in hell if it's what I have to do to keep you two together."

Pandora voice rumbled from Katie's throat. "So it is spoken, so shall it be..."

AUTHOR NOTES - MICHAEL ANDERLE

WRITTEN JUNE 1, 2018

First, THANK YOU for reading through this story to the back, here in the author notes .

Second, I'm writing these notes mere hours from release, so if there are any spelling errors, punctuation errors or just errors in general I'm going to blame the lateness of the night and all sorts of paranormal creatures.

Because I'm in New York City, home of the Ghost-Busters!

I'm on the downward slope to 51 years old, and I've visited New York more in the last 2 years of my life, than the previous 48. Each time I come here, I see a little more of the city, and recognize places I've seen in the movies shot here.

So, when it comes time to blame something or someone about my author notes, I can only imagine that little green Slimer has been doing some editing on my luscious prose.

<no I haven't.>

However, we all realize that the paranormal isn't real

<bite me, author man> and as an adult, we don't look under our beds at night anymore

<you should, I'm going to gnaw on your leg like a hungry Chihuahua stupid author man.>

Eight Stories in less than 90 days.

We just finished dreaming up, writing, editing, building covers, JIT teaming, and releasing eight stories in less than 90 days.

Oh, and the first audio book is out, as well! I have it on good authority she enjoyed narrating Pandora.

<That Emily Beresford is a riot. I think I'd like to possess her. I bet I make her laugh when she reads this.>

I would like to thank the fans for supporting this series, the JIT team for last minute edit checks, Lynne and company for editing our stuff, Laurie and team(s) on her side for collaborating (Laurie has her own complete support team for her writing, like I do), Stephen Campbell (Zen Master Walking ™) for building files and working corrections, Jude and Loraine on covers and my other collaborators for supporting me in all ways.

<you are a horrible blowhard author man. What the hell do you do if you have so many people help you?>

Plus, a SPECIAL shout out for those fans who are in the Protected By The Damned Facebook Group. Your constant fun, donut jokes, and Pandora snark helped keep me sane trying to take on such a large effort.

<author man stuck in the link to the Facebook Group...I deleted it. This was not an edit – I just stole the link and won't give it back.>

In the space of just 90 days, we created a new Universe, supplied it with stories and characters, drew together fans who loved this crazy-ass stuff we write and are now supporting us as we dig a little deeper and write more.

Just, perhaps, maybe on a slightly less chaotic schedule and slow down just a bit.

Or will we?

<I'm already getting my red-hot poker to brand his balls when he goes to sleep. He will be typing this shit standing up for months...>

I look forward to seeing you in Katie and Pandora's next series, WAR OF THE DAMNED.

Ad Aeternitatem,

Michael Anderle

<are you still reading this? Then you should know I'll be under your bed when the lights go out. Except for you Tomas Littleton (false advertising with the name there, Tomas) in Spokane Washington because I'd be scared you would break the bed and flatten me.>

Book 8. Book EIGHT! Can you believe it? How in the world are we already at book eight?

Time flies when you're having fun, I guess.

Hey! How are ya? Thanks for reading these author notes. I feel like we're seriously getting to know each other at this point in the game.

So, this last book was a boob buster. Boobs are rather universal, right?

So many things came out in this story, my FAVORITE one being Pandora's true identity. How freaking cool was that? I love it.

And the fun isn't over. Now that Protected by the Damned has wrapped up, Mike and I are pushing into War of the Damned, and I'm not sure if he told you this, but we're working on three (THREE) top secret projects related to the World of the Damned.

Things are getting exciting over here—in the book world at least.

In other news… Summer is in full effect here in Houston, and we are sweating outside. Inside. On the side. By each other's sides. It's hot as Hades here.

Hubs and I have a few more months in the lovely humidity, and then we're packing up and going Nomad for another year. We thought we were buying in Austin, but decided we wanted one more year on the road, so Northeast, watch out. Here we come.

As this first eight book story arc comes to a close, I just wanted to say thank you again. We appreciate you reading our stories and hope that they give you a laugh, a cry, or a good reason to be a writer—to save the world from us?

Anyway. Appreciate you, and look for a lot more coming from Mike and me. We're cooking up all sorts of great tales to fill your day with laughter if nothing else.

Slave to Many Stories,

Laurie Starkey